"There's someth you," she said.

Gabriel held up his ha[...], it's all water under the bridge. There's really nothing we have to talk about after all this time. Anything you want to say should have been said years ago."

When he'd wanted to talk things over with her three years ago, Rachel's response had been to skip out on him a few days before their wedding. She'd left him nothing more than a hastily scribbled note saying she couldn't marry him. All attempts to reach her had been rebuffed. She had effectively cut him out of her world.

"It's really important." Her brown eyes beseeched him to listen. The sense of urgency in her tone couldn't be ignored.

Suddenly, a sharp cry rang out from the other room. Rachel shut her eyes and let out a groan. More cries followed. It sounded like a baby wailing. Was Helene blasting the television? He didn't even remember there being one in the living room.

A funny feeling washed over him. All of his nerve endings were on fire. The sounds appeared to be growing louder by the second. "What is that noise?" he asked.

Rachel bit her lip. "I didn't come here alone, Gabriel. I brought my babies with me."

Belle Calhoune grew up in a small town in Massachusetts. Married to her college sweetheart, she is raising two lovely daughters in Connecticut. A dog lover, she has one mini poodle and a chocolate Lab. Writing for the Love Inspired line is a dream come true. Working at home in her pajamas is one of the best perks of the job. Belle enjoys summers in Cape Cod, traveling and reading.

Books by Belle Calhoune

Love Inspired

Home to Owl Creek

Her Secret Alaskan Family
An Alaskan Twin Surprise

Alaskan Grooms

An Alaskan Wedding
Alaskan Reunion
A Match Made in Alaska
Reunited at Christmas
His Secret Alaskan Heiress
An Alaskan Christmas
Her Alaskan Cowboy

Reunited with the Sheriff
Forever Her Hero
Heart of a Soldier

An Alaskan
Twin Surprise

Belle Calhoune

LOVE INSPIRED
INSPIRATIONAL ROMANCE

LOVE INSPIRED®
INSPIRATIONAL ROMANCE

Recycling programs
for this product may
not exist in your area.

ISBN-13: 978-1-335-48816-9

An Alaskan Twin Surprise

Copyright © 2020 by Sandra Calhoune

This edition published by arrangement with Harlequin Books S.A.

For questions and comments about the quality of this book,
please contact us at CustomerService@Harlequin.com.

Love Inspired
22 Adelaide St. West, 40th Floor
Toronto, Ontario M5H 4E3, Canada
www.Harlequin.com

Printed in U.S.A.

Thy word is a lamp unto my feet,
and a light unto my path.
—*Psalm* 119:105

For my brother, Eric Calhoune. Your love and support have always meant the world to me.

Acknowledgments

For all of my readers: I'm so grateful for your continued support and enthusiasm.

A special thank you to my editor, Emily Rodmell, and senior editor, Melissa Endlich, for allowing me to write this story.

Chapter One

Rachel Marshall had been dreaming about her return to Owl Creek, Alaska, for a very long time. It had been an eternity since she'd felt this arctic wind whipping against her cheeks and smelled the crisp, pure Alaskan air. Way too much time stood between her and this town, she thought, as regret sliced through her. It had been three years since she'd fled her hometown and made a life for herself in Colorado. Even now it seemed hard to believe that she'd taken off two days before her wedding. Back then she'd allowed fear to rule her life.

Rachel hadn't expected to feel this strong rush of emotion with regard to coming home, but it had hit her like a ton of bricks the moment she'd seen Anchorage from the airplane. Her chest had tightened as the rugged mountains and stunning landscape came into view. Then her pulse had quickened once she'd caught sight of the breathtaking harbor as the ferry steamed toward Owl Creek. Alaska! *Home.* A place like no other in this world.

Truthfully, it had been an exhausting journey from Denver. She'd avoided taking a seaplane from the Anchorage airport, knowing if she'd done so the news of her return would spread like wildfire through Owl Creek. She had no interest in fanning the flames of gossips. And besides, she didn't like flying on small planes. They reminded her too much of darkness and the loss of her father. Instead, Rachel opted for the ferry, which had been a bit of a challenge with two little ones to consider. The twins hadn't slept a wink ever since Anchorage, and then as soon as they'd reached Owl Creek, both girls had fallen fast asleep.

All of a sudden, her breathing became shallow. Raw emotion washed over her. She'd never once imagined returning to her hometown under these grim circumstances. Letting out a deep breath, she reminded herself of the reasons she'd chosen to come back home and take a leave of absence from her nursing position at Memorial General Hospital. Her mother's illness. Her duty as a nurse. Mama needed her. Now more than ever.

"I'm not doing so well, Rachel. Doc said the cancer is spreading." Once her mother had said those words to her she'd immediately made arrangements to come home to Owl Creek.

Helene Marshall was a proud woman who'd never asked for much in the way of help.

This time was different though. Her mother knew it was the only thing that made sense. Her illness was worsening, and she couldn't afford to hire a round-the-clock nurse to see to her needs.

Rachel had known she couldn't ignore her familial

obligations despite the fragmented relationship between her and her mom. She'd already lost so much. Losing her mother would be a devastating blow. It would be far worse if she didn't have the opportunity to care for her and to try and bridge the gap between them.

By the time she reached her mother's house, Rachel was completely exhausted.

She stood a few feet away from her childhood home and gazed at the modest ranch-style abode as memories washed over her. There had been such good times spent in this house. Most of those wonderful moments had ended right along with the premature death of her father. For Rachel it had seemed as if all the light was extinguished from her world when Lance had left them so suddenly. It still caused an ache of sadness and grief to overwhelm her. She shook off the melancholy emotions, choosing instead to focus on the here and now. She would need strength for what was to come. As a nurse she was accustomed to working with sick and dying patients, but caring for her mother would be far more personal than usual.

Rachel dug into her purse and pulled out the gold house key. She performed a juggling act as she let herself in, all while dealing with two sleeping babies in car seats. She put one carrier down inside the threshold, then pushed the other one in with her foot. A feeling of exhilaration soared through her. She'd done it! The girls had been premature babies and were still smaller than most one-year-olds. Nevertheless, lugging them around in their car seats was still an effort. Despite the complexities, she had made it all the way from Denver to her remote Alaskan hometown with her daughters.

Once she'd made it inside the house with the girls, she immediately called out to her mother. "Mama! It's Rachel. I'm home." Saying the words left her throat feeling clogged with emotion. She would never be able to put into words how much she'd missed being in this very place and how badly she'd wanted to return home. Despite all of the hard times she'd endured in this house, it fit her like a second skin.

"I'm in here!" her mother responded in a feeble voice. Rachel cringed at the sound of it, bracing herself at the prospect of coming face-to-face with her mother after all this time.

When Rachel had left Owl Creek her mother had been robust and healthy. Now, Helene was facing a seemingly insurmountable illness. She walked toward the sound of her mother's voice, heading into the spacious family room. Rachel sucked in a sharp breath at the sight of her sitting in a rocking chair by the window. Although Helene was a beautiful woman, cancer had left an indelible mark on her. Her cheeks were slightly sunken in and dark shadows rested beneath her eyes, no doubt due to her decreased appetite and restless nights.

"I've been waiting for you all day!" her mother said, scowling at her. Clearly she had seen their arrival from her bird's-eye view of the front yard. Rachel sighed. She couldn't tell whether her mother was pleased by their presence or not. Helene had always been hard to read and impossible to please. Swallowing her nerves, Rachel quickly moved toward her mother and placed a kiss on her temple. Helene reached up and smoothed her palm across Rachel's cheek. It was something she'd been doing ever since she was a small child, yet it surprised her to feel the slight caress. It had been ages since she'd experienced it.

"They're pretty little girls," her mother said in a begrudging tone as she gave the babies the once-over, her expression stoic. "Which is which? You've barely sent me any pictures of them at all."

"Thank you," she murmured, deciding to hold her tongue rather than remind her mother of their fractured relationship. Helene had a bad habit of only remembering the things she chose to recall. A quick glance around the room revealed not a single picture of the twins was on display. Rachel tried not to let it bother her.

"This is Faith in the pink and Elizabeth is wearing the mint-green coat. I call her Lizzy."

Pride rang out in her tone. She held so much love in her heart for her daughters. When she'd given birth to them, Rachel had vowed to never let anything come between her and her girls. And she never would.

"No one here in town knows about the twins," Helene said, locking gazes with Rachel. Her voice took on a wary tone. "It will come as quite a surprise to most folks when they see you with them."

Her mother's words served as a none-too-subtle warning. The townsfolk would be stunned by her return to Owl Creek with twin babies in tow. Not a single person would forget the manner in which she'd fled town three years ago. And she would face judgment in some circles for being an unwed mother.

It wasn't shocking at all to Rachel that her mother had sought to hide the existence of her grandbabies. Helene Marshall had always been very concerned about wagging tongues and gossip. Ever since Rachel could remember, she'd carefully guarded the reputation of the Marshall family to ensure their good name remained intact. Rachel had once cared about those things, but as a single mother raising twins, she no longer had time to worry about it.

"Well, that very well may be the case, but I'm not going to hide away from prying eyes," she said, her chin trembling. "I'll never regret these two little blessings." Nothing could ever make her feel ashamed of her sweet darlings despite the circumstances of their birth. Not even her mother's disapproval.

Helene just stared at her and said nothing further. Rachel knew her pursed lips meant she wasn't pleased by her daughter's response. In the past she'd hardly ever brought her mother a sense of pride. Rachel had always been lacking in Helene's eyes, and it still caused a world of hurt to rise up inside her. Even with an RN degree, Rachel still felt unworthy. In the past few years she had tried to better herself by dedicating her life to her profession and the girls. She wondered if her mother would even notice.

The peal of the doorbell startled Rachel, dragging her out of her thoughts.

"Go answer the door, Rachel. I'm expecting a delivery!" Helene barked.

Rachel darted a glance at Lizzy and Faith. "I'll watch the girls for you," her mother said. "I don't think they'll wake up. They both look plum tuckered out." A quick glance at the twins confirmed that they were still sound asleep in their carriers. They couldn't look more content.

Rachel let out a sigh at Helene's tone. Some things never changed. Her mother was still as sharp-tongued and dictatorial as ever. She quickly made her way to the front door and pulled it open. When she saw who was standing there, Rachel let out a gasp that echoed in the silence. All of sudden a feeling of unease gripped her. Even if someone had warned her, she wouldn't have been prepared for this cataclysmic moment.

Lord, help me...

"Gabriel!" The name flew out of her mouth. It had been so long since she'd uttered his name. It almost sounded foreign to her ears. For the better part of three years, Rachel had forced herself not to think about him. It brought her too much pain to dwell on what might have been if she hadn't run away from Owl Creek due to her fear of losing him in a plane crash. Gabriel's mouth was open, but he didn't say a word. His soulful brown eyes did all the talking for him. They radiated shock and confusion at the sight of the woman who'd left him in the lurch two days before they were supposed to get married.

Gabriel Lawson felt as if his legs might give out underneath him. For a moment he struggled to catch his breath. His ex-fiancée, Rachel Marshall, was standing mere inches away from him, looking even more beautiful than he remembered. With her warm brown skin, dark wavy hair and russet-colored eyes, she had always been a striking woman. The most beautiful girl in Owl Creek. His chest tightened as the weight of this moment settled over him. Seconds ticked by as he drank her in.

Words were lost to him. It felt as if someone had kicked him in the gut.

"Rachel." Somehow he managed to speak past his shock and confusion. Their eyes met and held. Neither one seemed able to look away from the other until a noise from down the hall jolted them both out of their stupor.

She waved him inside the house, and he walked in as if on autopilot. No one had told him about Rachel's return, least of all, her mother, Helene Marshall, who he saw a few times a week. A hundred different thoughts careened through his mind. Why had she come back to Owl Creek after all this time?

"W-When did you get home?" He blurted out the question as his mind whirled with a dozen or so more inquiries he wanted to hurl at her. All things considered, this seemed like a safe thing to ask.

"A little while ago," she answered in a low voice. "It was a long trip from Denver."

She was shifting from one foot to another and casting nervous glances over her shoulder. Denver! So that's where she'd landed. He'd heard rumors about her whereabouts on more than a few occasions. Hawaii. Seattle. Wyoming. Her mother had always remained tight-lipped on the subject, seemingly unwilling to disclose such information to Gabriel. After a while he hadn't even wanted to know such detailed facts about the woman he'd been desperate to forget.

"Who flew you in?" he asked, battling feelings of betrayal. He knew everyone in the local plane community, and he couldn't think of a single one who wouldn't have given him a heads-up regarding Rachel's return. They wouldn't have wanted him to be blindsided in this manner since everyone in town knew their tangled history.

"We flew to Anchorage, then took the ferry over," she explained.

We. The word immediately put him on edge, causing his body to stiffen. Had Rachel come back with a husband or a fiancé? Despite his frequent trips to her childhood home to bring Helene medicine and groceries, they never talked about the woman he'd once planned to marry. Rachel had always been a taboo topic of conversation, and he had no idea whether she'd moved on in her life and found the happiness he hadn't been able to give her. Frankly, he didn't *want* to know. She was a part of the past he'd been trying to stuff down for the last few years.

"So, what brings you here?" Rachel's gaze drifted toward the bag he was holding in his arms. She seemed nervous. He imagined she was feeling just as awkward as he was.

"I've been bringing supplies by and taking your mom to appointments when I can swing it," he explained. Unfortunately, he hadn't been of much help lately due to his hectic work schedule. But moving forward, he intended to spend a lot more time here due to his promise to help Helene with a home-renovation project. However, that might prove to be incredibly awkward due to Rachel's unexpected presence at the house.

Her expression registered surprise. "That's really nice of you. The two of you were always so close. Mama didn't mention a word about it though." She knitted her brows together, as if trying to process the information he'd just provided.

He shrugged. "It's the least I could do. She has a few friends stopping by along with Pastor Zeke and the visiting nurse, but it must get lonely out here since she's all by herself."

Rachel visibly bristled. He'd only been stating the facts, but his words were probably sounding like judgment to her ears. He had unwittingly poked at a sensitive subject.

"I only recently found out she was sick. She didn't tell Neil either. I came as soon as I could make plans to take leave from my job and sublet my condo."

Gabriel nodded. "I'm sure she's grateful. She'd never admit it, but I think she's missed you a lot."

"You're right about that," Rachel muttered under her breath. "She would never say those words to me in a million years."

Gabriel kept quiet. He had no intention of getting involved in any drama that might break out between Rachel and Helene. In the past he had refereed a multitude of misunderstandings and squabbles between them. Amidst all the dysfunction he'd always known there was tremendous love. Otherwise, Rachel wouldn't be standing here right now.

"Well," he said, letting out a deeply held breath, "I

should bring these things to her. Is she in the living room?" Rachel nodded, then reached out and held on to the sleeve of his coat.

"Gabriel. There's something I should tell you," she said, her tone sounding urgent.

He held up his hand. "Rachel, it's all water under the bridge. There's really nothing we have to talk about after all this time. Anything you want to say should have been said years ago. I just swung by to bring these items to Helene and chat with her for a bit."

Bitterness whipped through him. When he'd wanted to talk things over with her three years ago, Rachel's response had been to skip out on him a few days before their wedding. She'd left him nothing more than a hastily scribbled note saying she couldn't marry him. All attempts to reach her had been rebuffed. She had effectively cut him out of her world. His devastation had been complete. Making matters worse, the entire town had pitied him. His sense of self-worth had plummeted, and it had been a long time before he'd been able to look folks in the eye. Whatever Rachel wanted to get off her chest was several years too late!

"It's really important." Her brown eyes beseeched him to listen. A shudder went through him. The last time she'd had this expression on her face had been after his plane crash. The sense of urgency in her tone couldn't be ignored.

Suddenly, a sharp cry rang out from the other room. Rachel shut her eyes and let out a groan. More cries followed. It sounded like a baby wailing. Was Helene blasting the television? He didn't even remember there being one in the living room.

A funny feeling washed over him. All of his nerve endings were on fire. The sounds appeared to be growing louder by the second. "What is that noise?" he asked.

Rachel bit her lip. "I didn't come here alone, Gabriel. I brought my babies with me."

Gabriel's eyes widened. She saw it all—shock, disbelief and complete, utter amazement etched on his handsome tawny-colored face. Her stomach felt tied up in knots.

"Your *babies*?" he asked, a frown marring his perfect forehead. He was clearly having a hard time absorbing her words despite the fact that the cries were increasing in volume.

"Yes, I have two little girls. And I really need to see to them," she explained before turning on her heel and making a beeline to the living room. By the time she entered the room her mother had picked up Lizzy and was rocking her on her lap. Faith was still in her carrier squealing up a storm. Rachel scooped Lizzy up from her mother's arms, unsure as to whether Helene had the strength to hold her.

"I was doing fine," her mother groused. "I wouldn't have dropped her."

"They're pretty sturdy babies. I didn't want to overtax you," she explained. It hadn't taken her mother long to complain. She wondered if Helene just enjoyed pushing her buttons.

"That sounded like Gabriel at the door. Where is he?"

Helene asked, craning her neck as her eyes focused on the entryway.

Rachel shook her head. She had the feeling her mother had known full well that Gabriel would arrive at the house and come face-to-face with her and the twins. Hadn't Gabriel mentioned he'd been coming by regularly? Surely his visit wasn't a surprise to Helene?

Rachel heard footsteps behind her. When she turned around, Gabriel was standing in the threshold looking extremely uncomfortable. He was shifting from one foot to the other with the bag still held tightly in his hands. His gaze was focused on the twins.

"Gabriel!" Helene called out. Her entire face lit up with joy. Rachel couldn't help but feel a little jealous. How she wished her mother would look at her with such blatant adoration. But growing up in Owl Creek along-side Gabriel had always made her aware of his status as the town's favorite son. Some things would never change, she realized. His goodness radiated like the sun.

"Good afternoon, Helene," Gabriel said, a hint of a smile playing at the corners of his mouth. He walked over toward her rocking chair and leaned down to give her a hug.

In the meantime, Rachel had picked up Faith so that her two girls were perched on both sides of her hips. Their cries had quieted so now they were both merely breathing heavily and making little noises. As a mother she knew instinctively that they had reached their limit for the day, having traveled thousands of miles to reach their destination.

"I'm going to have to fix them something to eat,"

she said in an attempt to fill the silence. "They're probably hungry."

Gabriel didn't utter a word. His steely gaze felt like laser beams. She imagined he was still in shock that she'd shown up out of the blue with two toddlers.

"Gabriel, those are my grandbabies. Faith and Lizzy," Helene said, smiling as she looked in their direction. "Aren't they beautiful?"

Gabriel nodded as he looked them over. He turned back toward Helene. "You never said a word about being a grandmother," he told her in a chiding tone. "And yes, they're lovely."

"It really wasn't my business to tell," Helene answered, her mouth set in a prim line. "The circumstances have been less than ideal. Rachel is raising these babies all by herself."

Rachel let out a shocked sound at her mother's bluntness. "Mama!" She felt her cheeks reddening with embarrassment. "Please stop talking as if I wasn't standing right here. You don't need to explain my life to anyone!" Not to mention she was speaking to Rachel's ex-fiancé, the man she'd once loved more than anything. The same man she'd run out on because she'd been too afraid to marry a bush pilot and run the risk of him dying in a plane crash like her father. If Rachel wanted to tell Gabriel about her life she was fully capable of doing so without her mother's interference.

Helene rolled her eyes and let out a huff of air in response.

"Sit down and stay a while, Gabriel," her mom suggested, patting the love seat next to her. "I'd love to hear about your latest bush-pilot adventures."

"I really can't stay. I need to get back to town," Gabriel said. Once again his eyes settled on Rachel and the twins. "I just wanted to drop off these things. I managed to track down those books you've been trying to find. I have them on order."

Helene clapped her hands together. "Oh, that's wonderful. I can always count on you, Gabriel."

"You've always been good to me, Helene. I'm just returning the favor. I'll see myself out," he said with a nod before beating a fast path out of the room.

Rachel didn't have time to say goodbye to him. She felt certain Gabriel had wanted it that way judging by the rapid speed of his departure. In a perfect world, she imagined he'd never wanted to lay eyes on her again. Yet here she was, showing up in their small Alaskan hometown with two toddlers and no wedding ring. She could only imagine what he thought of her.

"I'll never understand why you didn't just go on and marry him." Helene made a tutting sound. "You'll never do better than Gabriel Lawson."

Although her mother's words might be true, they still caused a sharp knifelike sensation to spread through Rachel's chest. Did Helene think she needed to have her nose rubbed in it? She already lived a life ripe with regret. She'd hurt a good man like Gabriel due to her own fears and anxieties. Ever since she'd left Owl Creek, Rachel had carried the weight of it on her conscience.

"Like you always told me when I was a child, it's in the wind, Mama. There's nothing I can do to change it now." She turned away from Helene and blinked back tears. "Would you like a snack or something to drink? I'm going to fix the girls something to eat."

"I'm fine. You go and get those babies taken care of," Helene instructed, her expression softening.

Rachel placed the girls down on the floor and reached for their hands before leading them down the hall toward the kitchen. In moments such as this it was nice that the twins were now able to walk. Although their steps were halting, they were getting the hang of using their legs to explore the world around them.

Just as they entered the kitchen, Rachel stopped in her tracks. A lump rose to her throat at the sight of the two high chairs sitting next to the kitchen table. Her mother must have ordered them in anticipation of her arrival. The sweet and loving gesture meant the world to her. She needed a bit of comfort at the moment and her mother's thoughtful gift enveloped her like a warm, cozy blanket.

The day had been filled with lots of ups and downs. Showing up in Owl Creek after such a long absence was a bit jarring to her senses. Nothing seemed to have changed, yet her own life was vastly different. It was only her first day back in town and she felt as if she'd been run over by a truck. Seeing her former fiancé had thrown her completely off-kilter.

Gabriel Lawson was the whole package. With his dark good looks, rugged frame and magnetic personality, he drew admiring stares wherever he went. Everyone adored him. And Rachel had been completely devoted to him, believing their futures would be forever entwined. But because of her own fears and the inherent dangers of Gabriel's job, everything had fallen apart right before their wedding.

Rachel couldn't identify all of the emotions churning around inside her right now. All she knew was that for the millionth time since she'd left Owl Creek, she wished she had handled things differently. Although she regretted the pain she'd caused Gabriel by running away, she didn't regret her decision. There was no way, then or now, she could live each day in fear of losing a husband in a horrific plane crash the same way she'd lost her dad.

Chapter Two

There was something about soaring up in the wild blue yonder that made Gabriel feel as if all was right in his world even when it wasn't. Being up in the air was truly the closest he'd ever felt to God in his entire life. For him, flying was about truth and belief. It allowed him to push past boundaries and seek out the extraordinary. It centered him when it seemed as if nothing made sense. As a bush pilot he went out into the wild and uncharted Alaskan territories, delivering supplies and taking passengers to rugged and untamed destinations.

But today was simply about freedom. He was living out the dreams he'd held dear since he was a small child.

It had been the perfect day to put Bessie in the air even though it was his day off. The sky was the color of a robin's egg. Snow-capped mountains and Sitka spruce trees greeted him when he looked down at the rugged terrain. The waters of Kachemak Bay glistened with the sun's rays bouncing off the surface. He was fairly certain he could spot some owls soaring down below.

They were graceful and precise as they hunted their prey. The lack of daylight in November meant that sunset would settle in later this afternoon in true Alaskan fashion. Sometimes he enjoyed being up in the air just in time to see the sun dip below the horizon.

Gabriel hadn't been able to stop thinking about Rachel. It had been shocking enough to come face-to-face with her after all this time, but the knowledge that she'd given birth to twins had left him reeling. The love he'd felt for Rachel had faded a long time ago, but he couldn't seem to rid himself of all their shared dreams. Kids had been a large part of their plans. Seeing her two gorgeous babies reminded him of everything he'd lost when she abandoned him.

And despite everything, it gnawed away at him.

Had he been such an awful prospect for a husband that Rachel hadn't been able to commit to forever with him? Had she fallen out of love with him before the wedding? Was it possible she'd run off to be with someone else? So many questions still lingered in his mind. A part of him still craved answers.

Gabriel. I'm so sorry, but I can't marry you.

His body tensed up as the words from Rachel's letter crashed over him in unrelenting waves. He hadn't thought about it in a very long time. It was dangerous to allow his mind to go back to that bleak period. During the really dark days after Rachel's desertion he'd battled a myriad of emotions—shock, denial, anger then finally acceptance. The only way he'd been able to endure the loss had been to bury those feelings and move on with his life. But now, with Rachel being back in Owl Creek, everything was rising to the surface.

He looked at his watch. It was time to head back to the hangar. He turned the plane around and began to descend bit by bit until the clouds were above him and he could see the land below. Within minutes he was landing the plane on the airstrip behind the hangar. He jumped out of the plane onto the tarmac and rushed toward the small building.

Flying provided a calming experience for him, but he had lunch plans with his two best friends, Connor North and Hank Crawford. Although Gabriel knew it would only be a matter of time before the news spread through town about Rachel's return, he wanted to alert his buddies to her arrival. He imagined they would both be pretty shocked by the news.

When he walked into the Snowy Owl diner, the smell of French fries and bison burgers rose to his nostrils. His stomach growled in appreciation of the delightful scents. Breakfast had been hours ago, and he was in need of sustenance and a good dose of camaraderie. Both would serve as salves to his uneasiness regarding Rachel's return.

"Hey, Gabriel." Piper Miller grinned at him from behind the counter. "Your partners in crime beat you over here." She winked at him. "They're sitting in your usual spot. I'll get some coffee sent over right away for you."

"Thanks, Piper," Gabriel said, smiling at Hank's younger sister. Piper had taken over the ownership of the diner after the death of her father, Jack. She was a sweet and beautiful young woman who had lots of pluck and grit. Because of his close relationship to Hank, she'd always felt like a kid sister to him.

Gabriel slid into the booth beside Hank. "Hey, guys. Sorry I'm late. I took Bessie up for a quick spin among the clouds."

"I thought you had the day off," Hank said. "You should have been sleeping in and relaxing. Your schedule has been crazy lately."

His buddy was correct in his assessment. Working as a bush pilot didn't allow for much downtime, but it was a well-paying job that left him feeling fulfilled and energized. Being a pilot was the only vocation Gabriel had ever wanted to pursue. He loved what he did for a living.

"It's relaxing. There's nothing more peaceful than being up in the clouds. I flew to Raven's Pass, then turned around and headed home." Sometimes Gabriel struggled to put into words how euphoric flying made him feel. Hopefully after all these years of friendship, Hank and Connor both understood that flying was an integral part of him.

Gabriel smiled up at the waitress who'd come over to fill up his mug with a piping-hot serving of coffee. "Thanks, Rose. It's just what I needed." Hank slid the cream and sugar in his direction and Gabriel added liberal doses of each to his coffee before taking a long, satisfying sip.

His friends' gazes met across the table. A strange, almost imperceptible look passed between them. Gabriel immediately sensed something was up. He'd known both of them since they were all in diapers. Neither one had the ability to pull the wool over his eyes. Not even on their best days.

Gabriel placed his hands down on the table. "Okay. Spill it. What's going on with you two?"

Connor cleared his throat. "Some news reached our ears that you might find unsettling. So you need to brace yourself," he instructed. He was fiddling with his fingers and not making eye contact.

Gabriel nodded. "Is it about Rachel being back in Owl Creek?"

Connor swung his gaze up. His blue eyes widened. Gabriel almost wanted to laugh at the stupefied expression etched on his face.

"You knew?" Hank asked with a frown. "Why didn't you say anything?" His expression was a mix between irritation and relief.

Gabriel let out a sigh. "I just found out yesterday. I went to drop some items off for Helene, and Rachel answered the door." He let out a brittle laugh. "You have no idea how shocked I was to see her back in town. It was surreal."

Hank sat back in the booth. "I can't imagine. It's been three years since she left, right?"

Gabriel was too embarrassed to admit it, but he could probably pinpoint the exact number of months she'd been gone. Although he wasn't in love with Rachel anymore, he still hadn't managed to move past their relationship. Coming face-to-face with her yesterday had only served to remind him of that fact.

"Yeah. Three years since the wedding that wasn't." Although he tried to inject some humor into his statement it fell flat. He of all people knew there wasn't anything remotely funny about being left in the lurch by one's fiancée. Hank and Connor had stood by him in the aftermath of Rachel's desertion. He didn't imagine either one would have much to say to her if they crossed paths with Rachel.

"You're better off," Connor grumbled. "She clearly wouldn't have gone the distance."

"I have to agree with Connor," Hank said with a nod. "You deserve to be with someone who's going to love you through thick and thin." Hank had a dreamy expression etched on his face. He had recently gotten engaged to Sage Duncan, the love of his life. She happened to be Connor's long-lost sister Lily, who had recently been reunited with the North family twenty-five years after she'd been abducted from their home in Owl Creek. From what Gabriel could see, Hank and Sage were blissfully happy. Sometimes when he least expected it, he felt niggling feelings of envy. To love and be loved was a beautiful thing.

Gabriel crossed his hands in front of him. "She didn't come alone." The words slipped past his lips.

"Don't tell me she got married and brought her husband along with her," Hank groaned.

Connor put his head in his hands and shuddered. "Man, that's rough. I'm sorry."

"No, it's not that. She has children. Babies. Twins."

Connor choked on his coffee and sputtered, spraying the liquid in Hank's direction.

"Hey! Watch it there!" Hank picked up his napkin and swiped at his face. He glared in Connor's direction.

Gabriel felt the heat of two pairs of eyes focused on him like laser beams.

"She has kids?" Connor asked. His eyes were nearly bulging out of his head.

"Yep. Twin girls. And she's not married. Not sure if she's divorced or what, but Helene said she's a single mother. It's a bit strange no one here in town ever mentioned it. I don't recall ever seeing a single picture of them at her house." Gabriel felt a tugging sensation in the region of his heart just saying the words out loud. He felt a pang realizing she'd lived out certain dreams without him. He didn't want to admit it even to himself, but it hurt.

Hank let out a low whistle. "Wow. That must've been a lot to wrap your head around."

"I guess it's not that shocking," Connor said. "She's allowed to move on with her life, but you must be reeling from it all."

Gabriel nodded tersely. He wasn't sure he'd fully recovered from the events of yesterday.

Despite his attempt to appear cool, calm and collected regarding the reappearance of his ex-fiancée, his heart hadn't stopped thumping wildly in his chest since the moment he'd seen her.

"No wonder people are flapping their mouths around town," Connor said with a grimace.

"She's given them fodder to chew on."

"I don't want anyone talking badly about her." Gabriel's tone was curt, brooking no argument. "I know it might seem strange, but I still feel protective about her." He wasn't sure his friends would understand, but he'd spent so many years loving Rachel he simply couldn't allow folks to tear her down. It wouldn't sit well with him at all. As a man of faith, he knew trashing someone wasn't honorable.

"I hope you know we would never do that," Connor said. "We may not approve of the way she ended things with you, but we don't want to see her hurt, especially when babies are involved."

"You're a good man, Gabriel Lawson," Hank said, reaching out and slapping him on the back.

"She came home to help out her mother. That's what matters," Gabriel said. "Helene needs her family around her at a time like this."

"So how do you plan to handle her being back in town?" Connor asked. "It might get a little bit awkward."

"We really don't have a good reason to cross paths," Gabriel answered.

Hank frowned. "Aren't you doing some work at Helene's house?"

Gabriel let out a groan. He'd conveniently put that out of his mind in an effort to convince himself that he wouldn't have to see much of Rachel during her time in Owl Creek. Helene was on a fixed income and with mounting health costs she wasn't able to afford a professional contractor. Due to the fact that his own father had taught him the ins and outs of his contractor business before he'd retired, Gabriel could work on Helene's home-improvement project with his eyes shut. He was performing the work for free as a favor to Helene. Her late husband had been the one to teach Gabriel the skills of being a pilot. He had taken him under his wing and inspired him to get his pilot's license at seventeen years old.

There was no way in the world he could ever bail on the project, but the very thought of seeing Rachel on a regular basis made his head pound.

Suddenly, Piper was standing at their table, her expression strained. "Is it true?" she asked, hurt ringing out in her voice.

Gabriel didn't bother to ask what she was talking about. He had known when he'd woken up this morning that the news of Rachel's return would spread like wildfire through Owl Creek. As the owner of the diner, Piper was privy to all the latest gossip. It had only been a matter of time before someone mentioned Rachel being back in town.

"Yes, it's true. I saw her yesterday when I brought Helene some supplies," he admitted. "She came back to help with Helene's care."

The line of Piper's mouth appeared harsher than he'd ever seen it before. Steam was practically coming out of her ears.

"Well, I suppose I shouldn't be surprised," she spit out. "Rachel left us like a thief in the night and her return is just as abrupt as her departure." She reached out and touched Gabriel on the shoulder. "I'm so sorry. You're the last person who deserves to be blindsided again."

Before he could say a word, Piper stormed away from their table.

Gabriel threw his hands in the air. "I wish everyone

would stop worrying about me. I'm fine," he grumbled. "I'll admit it was a surprise to see her, but I'm not shattered."

"I should go see if Piper's all right. My little sister grieved the loss of their friendship when Rachel left town. She really loved her," Hank said with a grimace. "Not to mention that Braden skipped town right before her."

A sheepish expression crossed Connor's face. "At least he's back for now." He shrugged. "Although he hasn't exactly told us how long he's staying."

Braden North, Connor's younger brother, had returned to town to meet Sage after she'd been reunited with the North family. For the last few years he hadn't spent much time in Owl Creek, choosing instead to travel all over the globe in pursuit of adventures. He and Piper had been best friends for years prior to his disappearing act.

Gabriel stood up so Hank could get out of the booth to catch up to his sister. He watched as his friend made it over to the counter in a few easy strides. Hank reached out and cradled an emotional Piper in his arms. He gently guided her into the kitchen and away from prying eyes. Gabriel let out a ragged sigh.

Piper wasn't the only one who'd adored Rachel. He'd loved her more than he could ever truly put into words. Although he had given her his heart, it clearly hadn't been enough. And for the life of him, Gabriel still wished he knew why she had left town and ripped his life apart in the process.

* * *

Heading into town was the ultimate act of bravery as far as Rachel was concerned.

Because it was her first foray into the heart of Owl Creek, she'd made the decision to leave the twins with her mother and Beulah North, the grand matriarch of Owl Creek. Beulah had happily agreed to help watch the girls since she was still expectantly waiting for her own grandchildren to make her a great-grandmother.

Beulah was a member of the North family who owned North Star Chocolates. They owned a chocolate factory in town along with a shop on Main Street. As a teenager Rachel had worked at the chocolate factory. It had been her first after-school job where she'd earned a paycheck. Beulah had taken Rachel under her wing and showered her with kindness and guidance. Other than her mother, Beulah had been the only person she'd communicated with during her absence from Owl Creek. The older woman had been very encouraging regarding Rachel coming back to Alaska to help Helene. Just knowing she had an ally in Owl Creek had made it possible for her to return.

"It will give me an opportunity to be in the presence of little ones while visiting with your mother," Beulah had said, appearing quite eager to act as babysitter for a few hours. Thankfully, both the girls were well-adjusted with regard to caregivers. Neither one skipped a beat when she'd left the house and kissed them goodbye. Even though they were only one-year-olds, they were resilient children. It made her feel as if she must have done something right in her child-rearing.

Her heart ached a little bit at the sight of the majestic mountains rising up to greet her like an old friend as she drove into the center of town. How many times had she gazed at this vista and known with a deep certainty that she belonged in Owl Creek? She'd never wanted to wander far from this Alaskan hamlet, but circumstances had made it impossible for her to stay. Fear had held her in its fierce grip and all of the decisions she'd made had been born of that emotion.

Ever since then she'd been determined to be braver. Stronger.

Driving down Main Street allowed her to get a glimpse of a few new shops that had cropped up in her absence. There was a coffee place called Java and a small toy store with an abundance of brightly colored items displayed in the window. She made a note to pick up a few of them for the girls so she could tuck them away as gifts for the holidays. Enjoying high tea at Tea Time had always been her favorite treat, but there was no way she could ever walk into the establishment owned by Gabriel's mother. Iris Lawson wasn't a member of the Rachel Marshall fan club. Not by a long shot.

Now as she walked through the doors of the Snowy Owl diner, Rachel braced herself for impact. This place held so many memories for her—all of them good ones. She'd enjoyed her first date with Gabriel here, as well as indulging in Saturday afternoon milkshakes at the establishment with her father. Her brother, Neil, had once worked at the diner. Her eyes immediately focused on the cherry-red jukebox and her heart constricted. How many times had Daddy selected their favorite songs and serenaded her as they enjoyed one-on-one time with each other? She'd give anything to share one last song with him.

Rachel's face flushed as she became the subject of numerous stares and whispers. Her body tensed up and she considered walking right back out the door. Courage, she reminded herself. Surely she still had some friends in her hometown. Not everyone was a foe.

She swung her gaze around the place and felt a jolt upon spotting Gabriel sitting in a booth with Connor North. His eyes locked with her own. She couldn't help but remember all the times they'd met up here for a date night or a study session when they were in high school. Rachel wondered if Gabriel had held on to those memories, as well.

Gabriel stood up from his seat and began walking in her direction. His hands were stuffed into the pockets of his cords, his gait relaxed as he reached her side within seconds. As usual, his presence packed a punch. She sucked in a steadying breath. *Lord, help me.*

Suddenly it seemed as if all eyes in the diner were focused on the two of them. Rachel knew by nightfall rumors would be circulating throughout the village about her and Gabriel.

"Hey, Rachel. How are you?"

"Hi, Gabriel. I'm doing all right." Just talking to him again and being in such close proximity caused butterflies to soar around in her stomach. Was it possible he'd grown even more handsome in the past few years?

"And the girls?" he asked, looking around them. "Did you bring them into town with you?"

"No, they're back at the house with Beulah and Mama. They're still a bit tired from traveling yesterday. I'm actually looking for Piper. Have you seen her?"

Gabriel's eyes widened. There was a slight tick in his jaw. "She's in the back with Hank. I'm not sure right now is a good time to talk to her."

She paused for a moment, taking in the telltale signs Gabriel was giving off.

"She knows I'm back in Owl Creek, doesn't she?" Although she was holding her breath waiting for his response, Rachel knew by his demeanor that Piper was none too happy about her homecoming. If she hadn't been such a chicken, she would have called her childhood friend last night and told her she was back. But Rachel had worried Piper would simply hang up on her rather than talk things through. This way, she'd figured, Piper would have to face her.

"Yeah, she's pretty upset. I think she figured you would have reached out to her."

Rachel made a face. "I keep walking into minefields. I can't seem to get anything right, can I?"

"Give yourself a break. You've been gone a long time. It's normal to experience a few hiccups."

Gabriel's kindness only served to make her feel guiltier about her actions. "That's awfully nice of you to say, considering the way I left town."

His expression hardened. "I wasn't giving you a pass for breaking my heart," he said in a gruff voice. "And honestly, I don't think I ever will."

Rachel saw the intensity brimming in his eyes. It caused her to shiver. She wrapped her arms around her middle in a protective gesture. Suddenly she felt tongue-tied. How could she ever adequately explain her actions? Sadly, she'd been so busy running away from Gabriel and all of her fears that she had never taken the time to talk to him in an honest and open manner. In short, she'd been a coward. They both knew it.

Although she'd come back home in order to assist her mother and oversee her medical needs, perhaps Rachel also had an opportunity to heal old wounds. Time had given her perspective. She'd lived a dozen lifetimes since they'd been together. Becoming a mother had given her courage. Perhaps she could make Gabriel understand why she'd left Owl Creek.

Something shimmered and pulsed in the air as they stood facing one another. It seemed as if time stood still and they were the only occupants of the diner. An awareness flared between them.

"Believe it or not, I've never forgiven myself for walking away from us," she said, finally finding the nerve to look him squarely in the eyes without flinching. "And honestly, I don't think I ever will."

Chapter Three

Gabriel broke eye contact and looked away from her, his gaze swinging toward the counter. Every instinct told her Piper was standing there. The hairs on the back of her neck stood on end. When she turned around, a feeling of joy mixed with trepidation fluttered inside her chest. Piper was standing behind the counter flanked by her older brother, Hank Crawford. The look on Piper's face made her want to cry. She looked nothing like the warm, loving friend she'd known and adored. Her arms were folded tightly around her chest while her expression was mutinous.

"Hey, there," Rachel said, trying to fill the silence with conversation even though she hadn't a clue as to how to bridge the gap between them.

Hank nodded at her, his expression shuttered. As town sheriff, he had always been a people person, warm and friendly. At the moment, however, he radiated disdain. Because of her relationship with Gabriel, they had once been friends. It made her sad to realize she'd burned those bridges a long time ago. He was one of Gabriel's best buddies, and as such, he probably thought she was a horrible person.

"Hank. Why don't we give them some space to talk?" Gabriel suggested, motioning for the other man to head back to the table with him.

Hank looked reluctant to leave Piper's side. He turned toward her and his sister sent him a slight smile. "Go on, Hank. I'm good." When Hank and Gabriel walked away, Rachel stepped toward the counter, all the while praying.

Dear Lord, please give me the strength to face my dear friend and show her how sorry I am for turning my back on her and this town. I promise to do better in all things.

She vowed not to look away from the hurt and anger in Piper's eyes. It was important to deal with this head-on, regardless of how uncomfortable it felt. "I thought I'd surprise Mama by bringing her a milkshake. She really loves them, especially chocolate and strawberry. These days it's important that she keeps up her strength." She let out a sigh. "Coming by also gave me an opportunity to see you." She bit her lip. "Actually, that's the real reason I'm here."

Piper's lip curled. "Me? Why? We haven't spoken in years." Piper tapped her finger against her chin. "Hmm. The last time I saw you I was being fitted for my bridesmaid dress. And then poof, you were gone without a single word of goodbye. You also weren't reachable by cell phone." She began slowly clapping. "Nicely done."

Rachel flinched. Ouch! Piper was putting all the

nitty-gritty details out there for everyone in close proximity to hear—she certainly wasn't pulling any punches. Rachel hated that their conversation was so public, but in order to win back Piper's friendship, she would suffer the scrutiny from the townsfolk.

"I'm so sorry about that, along with a hundred other things," Rachel said.

Piper's nostrils flared. "You should be. We were friends! You were the older sister I never had. I honestly thought you hung the moon until you took off."

"I know you're angry at me! And I totally deserve it. I was broken and confused when I left here. I failed to do what was right and I hurt a lot of people in the process. But I'm back to help Mama through her illness. And to try to make amends if it's at all possible." Her voice cracked and she knew she was seconds away from breaking down in a torrent of tears. It hurt so much to realize how many people she'd wounded. She refused to allow this to be her legacy—pain and hurt. "I want my girls to be proud of their mother. I want to be a better person than I used to be."

Piper's lips trembled. "I can't believe you have baby girls." Her tone had softened.

"Me neither," Rachel said, laughing through her tears.

"You always did say you wanted a houseful of them," Piper recalled, a half smile tugging at her lips. "You're almost there."

Rachel grinned. It was lovely to hear someone speaking positively about her children.

Piper's words reminded her that becoming a mother

had been her most fervent wish, along with becoming Mrs. Gabriel Lawson and getting her RN degree. Although her matrimonial dreams had gone up in smoke, God had delivered her heart's desire by giving her Lizzy and Faith.

Rachel wiped away a tear from her cheek. "I want you to meet them. I'm pretty biased, but they're fairly incredible, just like their honorary auntie." Piper and Rachel had promised each other long ago that they would become aunties to each other's children. If Piper allowed it, she fully intended to honor the commitment. Her daughters would greatly benefit by having a strong, caring woman like Piper in their lives.

Piper let out a cry and came from behind the counter, reaching out to Rachel with open arms. She enveloped her in a tight bear hug. After a few moments, Rachel said, "Piper, you better let me go. I—I can't breathe."

Her friend let her go and they both cracked up laughing. Piper was effusive in everything she did. It was one of the main things she loved about her. She knew how to live life out loud. Not having the benefit of her friendship over the past few years had left a huge void in Rachel's life. She prayed they could get back to the days where they would finish each other's sentences.

Piper made a face. "I have to get back to work, but we need to get together soon. I can't wait to see those precious girls." She lowered her voice. "You owe me some answers."

Rachel nodded. "I know, Piper. And you'll get them. I promise."

"And I'll whip up that chocolate shake for you," she said with a wink.

Rachel let out a sigh of relief as she sat down at the counter and waited for her mother's treat. She was happy she'd taken the leap of faith and come to the Snowy Owl diner today. It hadn't been easy to face Piper, but in order to walk a righteous path she knew she would confront obstacles and awkward situations. She'd done enough running.

Her mother's illness brought everything into perspective. She had to live each day to the fullest and seek out the forgiveness she knew she might not deserve, but that she truly wanted in order to move forward in her life. Tomorrow wasn't promised. She needed to make things right with everyone she'd harmed. And Gabriel was at the top of her list.

"Why don't you just go over there?" Connor asked, looking across the table at Gabriel. "You can't seem to stop staring at them." He took a big bite of his bison burger and let out a satisfied sound.

"And you're wasting a perfectly good salmon melt and cheddar fries," Hank said, nodding in the direction of Gabriel's plate. "I never thought I'd see the day when you didn't scarf down your lunch."

"Well, I'm not the only one looking," Gabriel muttered. "Everyone in here is gawking at them as if their lives depended on it. Their conversation will probably be detailed in the *Owl Creek Gazette* word for word."

"It's not your place to worry about it. Don't let Rachel's return drag you under," Hank warned. "Connor and I both remember how gutted you were after she left you. There were days when it was hard for you to get out of bed."

Gabriel knew he was probably blaming the messengers, but he was feeling a bit annoyed at his best friends and their all-knowing comments. Did Hank actually think he had forgotten the agony he'd endured at the hands of his ex-fiancée? To this day Gabriel still had nightmares where he was standing at an altar in an empty church looking around for his missing bride-to-be. When he least expected it, Gabriel always came across some old memento from their time together. Ticket stubs. A photograph. A birthday card with her sweet words and signature inside. He hadn't forgotten a single thing, even though he wished he could.

He gritted his teeth and slowly counted to ten in his head. "I'm not likely to forget what she put me through, Hank, and I have no intention of allowing myself to get swept up by Rachel's beauty and charm. Been there, done that."

"Well, it looks like they're friends again," Connor said matter-of-factly. "Raised voices. Hugs. Laughter. A few tears. And all is forgiven."

"It's not that simple," Gabriel gritted out. "Even if your head urges you to forgive someone, your heart might have a hard time doing so." He reached into his pocket and slapped some bills down on the table. "I'm going to head home. I've lost my appetite. See you guys later."

Gabriel got up from the table and walked away. He knew his mood was all over the place, so there was really no point in putting on a smile and pretending as if his head wasn't about to explode. He'd done that for way too long now and it hadn't done anything to help him heal. Although he heard his buddies calling his name, he simply raised a hand in farewell and kept moving toward the exit.

He headed outside and zipped up his parka, bracing himself for a blast of cold air. The temperature today was a frigid sixteen degrees. As he made his way to his car, Gabriel caught a glimpse of Rachel walking ahead of him. He knew it was her, due to the bright pink coat she was wearing along with a matching hat. It had always been her favorite color, and clearly that hadn't changed.

He really couldn't win today. Despite his best intentions to stay far away from his ex-fiancée, Rachel seemed to be everywhere.

At the moment Rachel was juggling a drink in her hand and searching inside her purse, presumably for her car keys. She was clearly struggling and leaning her hip against the truck for balance. Force of habit caused him to make a beeline to her side in order to help her out. He hadn't even realized she'd left the diner and now he was rushing to her rescue as if he was Sir Galahad. Was this how it was going to be for the duration of her stay in Owl Creek? Would it be impossible for him to steer clear of her?

"Need some help there?" he asked when he was within a few feet of her.

Rachel swung her gaze up, a look of relief sweeping across her face as she laid eyes on him. "Thanks. I'm about to drop this milkshake, which would be a real shame for Mama. Can you grab it?" Gabriel stepped in and rescued the drink before it slid from her hand. Rachel then dug into her purse and held the keys up with a triumphant cry.

"How did it go with Piper? I couldn't help but notice the two of you seemed to have patched things up by the end of your talk." Maybe he was prying, but their conversation had been on full display for all of the diner's customers. It wasn't exactly a state secret.

Rachel gifted him with a sweet smile that lit up her entire face. "It's going to take some time to get back to where we used to be, but I really think we can move forward. Piper's heart is as wide as Kachemak Bay. It always has been." She shook her head ruefully. "I feel very blessed."

He could see a major difference in her demeanor between earlier and right now. It was as if a huge weight had been lifted off her chest by making peace with Piper. Gabriel wasn't certain why he still cared about Rachel's happiness, but it meant something to him to see her so pleased.

A burst of anger rose up inside him. Why was he being so kind to the woman who had kicked his heart around like a football? He needed to listen to Hank's warnings about getting tangled up again in Rachel's web. Perhaps this was the perfect opportunity to let her know where things stood between them. For now and for always. Maybe if he set her straight, he wouldn't feel so unsettled around her.

"I wanted to tell you I'm going to be hanging out

at your mom's place a lot in the next few weeks. I'm doing some work on a home-improvement project she asked me to help her with a few months ago," he explained. "I agreed to help out before I knew you were going to be here."

Rachel's brows were furrowed as she looked at him. "Okay. And? I'm not sure why you're telling me this. Are you going to be making a lot of noise or something?"

"Hopefully not, although I'll definitely keep it to a minimum so I won't disturb your kids." He shifted from one foot to the other, trying to find the words to make sure the lines between them were established. "I didn't want you to think I was coming around to see you, because that's not the case. I made a promise to Helene and I plan to fulfill it. That's it, plain and simple," he explained in a curt voice.

Perhaps he was imagining it, but the color of Rachel's eyes seemed to deepen as he spoke, going from a russet to a mahogany. It was a sure sign he'd angered her. He couldn't help but notice her jaw tightly clenching.

"Gabriel, I have no illusions about the two of us. My main focus in my life these days is my children. And seeing Mama through her illness. My plate is really full at the moment." She reached out and took the milkshake from his hands. "We ended a long time ago. I think it's safe to say we both know there's nothing between us but the past." She ran a shaky hand through her long mane of hair. "I really should get going. I need to run to the pharmacy before I head back home. I've been away too long already."

She turned back toward her truck and got behind the wheel. He stood by and watched as she revved the engine and roared off toward the other end of Main Street. There was no disputing the fact that he'd ruffled her feathers.

He should feel better for having set things straight with Rachel. But he didn't. There was still an ache in his soul the size of Alaska. She'd made him feel rather foolish for his comments, as if he thought her world revolved around him. But Gabriel had no delusions about Rachel's feelings. She had made it abundantly clear she had no use for him when she'd hightailed it out of town rather than spend a lifetime with him.

Rachel drove down Main Street and headed toward Doc's pharmacy to pick up a few personal items for Helene. She also needed fingernail polish, polish remover and cotton balls so she could do her mother's nails tonight. Rachel wanted to pamper her a little bit since she had the feeling it had been a very long time since she'd gone to the hairdresser or nail salon. As a nurse she knew how important it was to keep up a patient's positive attitude and appearance.

At the moment, however, she was having a fierce conversation with herself about Gabriel Lawson.

Did he really think she would be so incredibly self-centered as to believe his presence at Mama's house revolved around her? Had he followed her out of the diner so he could set her straight?

She wondered if he'd ever truly known her. They'd

once been true kindred spirits, completely head over heels in love with each other.

There hadn't been a doubt in Rachel's mind about their shared future until Gabriel's plane crash. Then it had all collapsed down around her. As a result, the terrifying memories of her father's fatal plane wreck had washed over her in unrelenting waves for weeks on end. Her sleep had been plagued by fiery nightmares, and fear had been her constant companion. She'd been convinced history would repeat itself and that Gabriel too would perish in a plane crash. Her attempts to talk to him about her fears had been dismissed. She'd soon come to the realization that Gabriel's number-one priority in the world had been his career as a pilot. Because of her fears, Rachel had pulled away from Gabriel emotionally in an effort to protect herself. In the weeks leading up to the wedding Rachel had felt very disconnected from her fiancé. Gabriel had been so distracted during that time she wasn't even sure he'd noticed her distant behavior. In the end, she'd taken off before their wedding, unable to bear the thought of losing yet another person she loved in such a devastating way.

"Rachel Marshall! Is that you?" She looked up to see an older white-haired gentleman smiling down at her. With his piercing blue eyes and round spectacles, Rachel would recognize him anywhere. Doc Johnson had owned the pharmacy ever since she could remember. He'd also been the occasional substitute teacher in her high school science courses. Through the years he had given her massive encouragement about becoming a nurse.

"Hey, Doc. It's great to see you." Rachel leaned in and gave him a hug. Doc wrapped his arms around her in a comforting embrace.

"How's the nursing going? I think it's wonderful how you achieved your dream of becoming a nurse." He shook his head. "I know it wasn't easy."

Rachel grinned. It had been a demanding road, but she felt a deep sense of pride in having gone the distance and obtaining her RN degree. It had taken her a total of five years, but it had been time well spent. Other than Lizzy and Faith, it was her greatest accomplishment. "No, it wasn't a cake walk, but I really enjoy helping people so it's been a great fit for me. I've been working in one of the biggest hospitals in Colorado."

"I'm not surprised at all, Rachel. You've always been determined to pursue a medical career. It's wonderful to see you back in town. Please give Helene my regards and tell her she's been in my thoughts."

"I certainly will, Doc."

He snapped his fingers. "By the way, there are lots of women in this town who would welcome the services of a midwife in case you're interested."

"Thanks, Doc. That's good to know." Small Alaskan towns such as Owl Creek suffered from a shortage of trained midwives. Rachel had both the experience and the credentials to deliver babies and serve in that capacity. She had completed her graduate degree in midwife nursing through an online program and had delivered dozens of babies. It was too bad she wasn't staying in town long-term. It would be fulfilling to be of service to women who needed help bringing their children into the world.

The exchange with Doc left her with a smile etched on her face as she headed outside into the Alaskan cold. Not everyone in town thought poorly of her. There were still some folks like Doc Johnson who remembered her fondly and were in her corner. It left her feeling invigorated. Hopeful.

Rachel rounded the corner and felt a solid presence crash into her.

"Oh, I'm so sorry—I didn't see you th—" The words died on Rachel's lips as she stared into the eyes of Iris Lawson. A chill swept through her. Iris was the last person she'd wanted to cross paths with in Owl Creek.

"Mrs. Lawson," she said, forcing herself to be cordial.

"Rachel. I just heard you were back in town." With her tall, thin frame, Iris was an elegant, well-dressed woman who exuded refinement. Although she'd always intimidated Rachel a bit, Gabriel's mother had always treated her warmly until she'd broken her son's heart.

Rachel nodded but kept quiet because she had no intention of politely conversing with the older woman. She could remember their last conversation so vividly it gave her goose bumps.

Iris's eyes radiated uncertainty. "Rachel, could we talk over tea? I have so much to say to you. You've been in my thoughts for quite some time now."

Every nerve ending in her body bristled. "I don't think so," she replied with a shake of her head. "You see,

I haven't forgotten all those hateful things you said to me the last time we spoke. Or the way you treated me."

Iris began wringing her hands. "I owe you an apology. What I did was wrong. I had no business keeping you and Gabriel apart."

"You did a little more than that, Mrs. Lawson. You kicked me when I was at my lowest point. I was in a very vulnerable state and you ran roughshod over me. There's no way you could ever understand what that did to me."

Tears pooled in Iris's eyes. "I imagine you won't fully understand, or perhaps you will since you're now a mother yourself. I was desperate to protect my son. The thought of you ripping his heart out again led me to act in a shameful manner. I've regretted it every day since then."

Rachel lifted her chin up. "I carry a lot of shame as well, but the one thing I know is that I never deliberately intended to hurt Gabriel or anyone else. I'm not sure you can say the same," Rachel said, moving away from Iris so she could end the conversation and head back home.

Iris reached out and grabbed Rachel's arm. The expression stamped on her face was one of pure panic. "Please don't tell Gabriel about what I did. He'd never forgive me."

Rachel shook herself away from Iris's grip, determined not to get locked into a battle of wills with Gabriel's mother. She turned away from Iris, tears burning her eyes as she made her way to her vehicle. Once she was safely inside, she allowed herself to cry.

Three years ago, she had run away from her wed-

ding and the only man she'd ever truly loved, out of
sheer terror. Weeks later her attempts to make things
right had been thwarted by Gabriel's own mother. Although she knew the time had come to explain things
to her ex-fiancé, there was no way she could disclose
Iris's role in the situation.

She'd already hurt Gabriel enough for one lifetime.
Revealing his mother's deception would be adding salt
to the wound. After everything that had happened between them, Rachel wasn't even certain Gabriel would
believe her.

Chapter Four

Gabriel let out a sigh as he inspected the wall in front of him. It wouldn't take much to knock it down, but he had to be certain there wasn't anything structural standing in the way that might present a problem. Helene's house had to be at least forty years old, he surmised. More times than not, old homes tended to have surprises when you started poking around. Pops had taught him well in the area of home construction, and he wasn't going to jump feet first into anything without taking the proper precautions. He would also have to hang up plastic sheets to prevent dust and allergens from circulating through the home, as well as asking Rachel to put baby gates up nearby so the girls would never venture into his work area.

Turning the den into a larger space all made sense now. Helene wanted to transform the room into a playroom for her granddaughters. It wasn't any of Gabriel's business, but he wasn't sure it was practical. Rachel wasn't moving back permanently to Owl Creek with her girls. From what he'd gleaned from their conversation, she was simply here to take care of Helene during her illness.

Gabriel knew fear when he saw it, and he couldn't help but sense Helene was afraid of medical procedures. He'd seen it before in small Alaskan towns where people lived their entire lives without ever going to the hospital for any type of emergency.

He wondered how much Rachel knew about Helene's diagnosis. For as long as he could remember, the two women had been at odds. Rachel had always chafed against her mother's rules, while Helene had withheld her approval from her only daughter. Losing Lance had been devastating for the entire family. He'd been the glue holding everyone together, and without his presence in their lives, the family dynamic had crumbled. Perhaps they would finally come together due to Helene's health battle.

Even though he'd prepared himself for the sight of Rachel and the twins as he arrived at Helene's house this morning, his insides were still all tied up in knots. It still felt surreal. He couldn't fathom why Helene had never mentioned such a huge development in her daughter's life. Perhaps she had been trying to be kind by not sharing the news.

It wasn't easy to pretend as if he didn't have a problem being in her vicinity. It felt like a scab that still hadn't healed. Every time he heard laughter from down the hall it made him wonder about Rachel's life in Colorado with the twins. Had she found happiness? She seemed to have a great rapport with her children. A woman like Rachel wouldn't have had any trouble finding male companionship. She'd always been the most beautiful woman in town.

A flash of red in his peripheral vision caught his attention. When he looked up, Rachel was standing a few feet away from him. Even dressed in a simple long-sleeved crimson top and a pair of jeans, she looked stunning. She'd swept her long hair up into a ponytail, making her look way younger than her twenty-eight years. Although his mind told himself not to stare at her, Gabriel couldn't help it.

Rachel shifted from one foot to the other. "Would you like some coffee or tea? We're about to sit down in the kitchen for a snack. I made some snickerdoodles."

Snickerdoodles! So that explained the delectable aroma emanating from the kitchen.

Rachel knew they had always been his favorite cookies. He couldn't count the number of times he'd sat at the Marshall's kitchen table and devoured freshly baked cookies and drank numerous glasses of chocolate milk. It seemed so long ago.

He didn't really want to sit down across a table from Rachel, but he figured it was Helene who'd requested his company. Whenever he stopped by to check on her, they would share a cup of tea and discuss all the goings-on in Owl Creek. It never failed to amaze him how Helene managed to keep up so well with town gossip despite being housebound.

"Sure," Gabriel said with a brusque nod. He didn't want Rachel to think his acquiescence had anything to do with her. Spending time in her company wasn't exactly on his to-do list. Things still felt incredibly tense between them, and it was hard to wrap his head around the fact that they'd once been inseparable and so deeply in love. Time, distance and Rachel's betrayal had severed their connection.

It wasn't the moment or the place, but he intended to confront Rachel about the past once the timing was right and they were alone without the possibility of being interrupted. Now that she was back, it provided the perfect opportunity for closure. Maybe then he'd be able to commit himself to another woman and settle down like he'd always wanted to. Gabriel had nurtured dreams of a wife and family for as long as he could remember. His personal life was still in shambles; his relationships never seemed to amount to anything more than a few dates. He'd gone out with a few women in Owl Creek, but he always seemed to lose interest before things developed. How could he even consider being in a committed relationship when his heart wasn't whole?

He looked down at his hands. They were covered with sawdust. "Let me just go wash up and then I'll join you," he said.

Rachel nodded, then turned on her heel and headed toward the kitchen. Judging by her rapid retreat, he sensed she wasn't in any hurry to spend alone time with him either. It was fine by him, he thought, as a rush of anger speared through him. He wasn't the one who'd been in the wrong. It hadn't been *his* decision to end the relationship. Other than a cursory note she'd left in her wake saying she was sorry, Rachel had never taken the time to apologize to him. And the antique sapphire and

diamond ring he'd lovingly placed on her ring finger
had been left behind, serving as a cruel reminder of his
crushed hopes and dreams. After all they had meant to
each other, it still burned a hole through him that she
hadn't thought him worthy of a face-to-face meeting.

By the time he'd washed up and made his way to the
kitchen, Helene and the twins were seated at the table
while Rachel was buzzing around putting bibs on the
girls and placing Cheerios and sippy cups in front of
them. Her movements were gentle. Maternal. Each gesture filled with love and care.

Faith and Lizzy were beautiful little girls. His heart
clenched as his gaze swept over them. With their round
cheeks and big brown eyes, they were the very image
of Rachel. She had brought two mini versions of herself into the world. He didn't even want to think about
their father, although he was curious about whether he
was still in Rachel's and the twins' lives. Helene had
emphatically stated Rachel's status as a single mother.
Gabriel knew he was reading between the lines, but it
didn't seem as if Rachel had any support. Had things
fallen apart between Rachel and the father of her twins?

It has nothing to do with you, he reminded himself
angrily. Rachel hadn't been his concern for a very long
time. He'd fervently believed she would be his forever,
but instead of marrying him, Rachel had turned into a
runaway bride. The shame and embarrassment of being
dumped days before saying their *I do*s still made him
feel like a world-class chump. All of his life he'd been
viewed as a good guy in his hometown, but Rachel

had walked all over him. *Nice guys finish last* was the phrase that always came to mind.

"What kind of tea would you like?" Rachel asked, pointing to the assortment in the middle of the table. Gabriel reached out and picked up a bag of chamomile. Thanks to his mother's tea shop, he knew a lot about different flavors. Chamomile was his favorite. A heaping plate of snickerdoodles was sitting in the center of the table. He eagerly helped himself to two cookies.

Rachel leaned over and poured hot water into his cup. He could smell a sweet fragrance hovering over her like a halo. Peaches and vanilla. Her signature scent. Just the aroma of it brought back a wealth of memories, ones he couldn't allow himself to savor.

Helene reached over and patted his hand. "I want to thank you again for doing all of this work for me. You're a good man." Her eyes darted toward Rachel.

Rachel cleared her throat. "It's very thoughtful of you, Gabriel."

He winked at Helene. "You know I'd do anything for you."

She giggled like a schoolgirl. "You're making me blush."

Gabriel noticed a tiny smile tugging at the corner of Rachel's lips. She had always appreciated the easygoing relationship he'd shared with Helene. When they were engaged, he'd looked forward to becoming a part of the Marshall family, never imagining how badly things would veer off course in the long run.

He looked over at the twins. So far, he'd tried his best not to let his eyes linger on them too long. His emotions were a bit all over the place with regard to Rachel's offspring. It was difficult for him to even process his feelings. Somehow the idea of Rachel having kids with another man had never even occurred to him. He watched as the girls began feeding each other cereal which drew laughter from Helene. A feeling of longing swept over him. For some time now he'd wanted a family of his own. It hit him every time he saw Hank with his baby girl, Addie. Now that Hank was set to marry Sage, Gabriel couldn't help but think his friend had everything he would ever need to make his life complete. He envied him.

"Look at that! They sure do love each other," Helene said, beaming as she looked at the baby girls. It was nice, Gabriel realized, to see Helene enjoying her grandchildren. It seemed to soften her hard edges. She'd never been the most effusive woman with her feelings. Rachel had never truly believed her mother loved her, largely due to Helene's sharp tongue and endless criticisms. He couldn't help but notice that Rachel was loving in each and every interaction with the twins. It didn't really surprise him, since he'd always known she would be a great mother.

"I've always heard that twins share an unbreakable bond. It looks as if these two are no exception," he said, marveling at their connection. They were so cute in their matching outfits and pigtails. God had doubly blessed Rachel.

Rachel smiled as she lovingly looked at her girls. "They're two peas in a pod. They are very different personality-wise, but I think it's safe to say they'll be best friends." She let out a sigh. "I hope they'll always have each other's back."

Gabriel thought of his own four siblings. Although his older sister Tabitha was the only one who still lived in Owl Creek, they were all still close. Growing up in a large, tight-knit family had always made him want to have his own big, bustling clan. At the moment it seemed as if that particular dream was way out of his reach. He'd have to settle for being an uncle to Tabitha's soon-to-be child, who was expected in a few weeks.

"And what about their father?" Helene asked with a raised brow. "Shouldn't he have their backs as well?" She paused to take a lengthy sip of her tea.

For a moment the table became very quiet. Tension flared in the air. Suddenly, Gabriel wished he'd declined the invitation to share afternoon tea with mother and daughter. Somehow he had forgotten how quickly things tended to spiral out of control between them. It was turning into an incredibly awkward situation.

Gabriel darted a glance in Rachel's direction. Her cheeks were turning pink. "Mama…please!" she said in a sharp voice. "I already told you, he's not in their lives or mine. He didn't want to be a father and he made it abundantly clear to me he had no intention of being a part of raising them." Her brows were knitted together as she shot Helene a glare. "It's not something I want to discuss any further. Anything the girls will ever want or need, I can provide for them."

Helene made a tutting sound. "What kind of man walks out on his children and doesn't take responsibility for the lives he created?" Gabriel was pretty much wondering the same thing, but he would never add fuel to the fire by saying so.

"That's enough, Mama," Rachel cautioned in a stern voice.

He could practically see the steam coming out of her ears. Helene was pushing her daughter to the point of no return. It would only be a matter of time before Rachel lost her composure. She was like a slow-heating kettle when it came to her emotions.

"I would love to know Gabriel's opinion on the matter," Helene said, her gaze focused on him like laser beams. She raised a questioning eyebrow in his direction.

"It's none of my business," he replied in a curt tone. He wasn't interested in being dragged into such a personal matter. Besides, Gabriel didn't want to know the nitty-gritty details of Rachel's love life. "If you'll excuse me, I really should be getting back to work." He abruptly stood up from the table and said, "Thanks for the tea. Much appreciated," before beating a fast path away from the kitchen.

With every step he took, he felt anger pulsing in his veins. He felt nothing but disgust toward any man who walked away from his responsibilities. Fatherhood was a precious gift. A blessing from God. Who wouldn't embrace it? It infuriated him for those two precious little girls who were innocent victims of their father's selfishness. Rachel's beautiful face flashed before his eyes. The thought of a man not wanting to be with her stunned him. For so long it was all he'd ever wanted or needed.

Life wasn't fair. He would have done anything, sacrificed it all to be with her. But she hadn't wanted him, had she? She'd chosen a different life for herself, one that had brought two beautiful babies into her world, along with a man who hadn't been built for the long haul. Gabriel didn't know why it bothered him so much. Rachel wasn't his woman anymore. Their lives were miles and miles apart from the days when they'd finished each other's sentences and shared their dreams under a sky full of stars.

Shouldn't a part of him feel satisfaction that she'd gotten burned after what she'd done to him? But the truth was, he didn't feel one ounce of pleasure in learning about Rachel's setbacks.

Matter of fact, it made him feel things he didn't want to face. Not today. Maybe not ever.

Rachel's face still felt warm with embarrassment. It had been mortifying to have her mother air her dirty laundry. What must Gabriel think? He already had every reason in the world to think poorly of her. This information surely only served to make her look worse in his eyes. She still felt a great deal of shame about Jonathan DeMarco walking away from her and the girls. Rachel had met Jonathan at a low period in her life. Away from her beloved hometown and estranged from Gabriel and most of her loved ones, Rachel had been completely adrift for a very long time. Over a year after her arrival in Denver when a few of her nursing friends invited Rachel to a night out at the rodeo to lift her mood, she'd met the handsome bull rider. She'd been swept away by his charm and good looks. In the long run, Jonathan hadn't been interested in home and hearth. He'd told her he wasn't the type to plant roots and wanted to travel around on the rodeo circuit. And when he discovered she was pregnant, he'd made it clear to her that he didn't want to be a father to the twins.

Helene wagged a finger in her direction. "Wipe that frown off your face. You're too pretty to scrunch up your features like that. You'll get wrinkles."

Rachel stopped gathering up the plates and met her mother's gaze head-on. "I have no idea why you brought up the subject of Jonathan in front of Gabriel."

Helene grumbled. "Why not? I think Gabriel would want to know you're as single as a dollar bill. Not to mention the fact that the girls don't have a father in the picture. He can have a ready-made family in a heart-beat."

Rachel felt her jaw drop. Had she heard her mother right? Was Helene attempting to play matchmaker?

"Are you joking?" Rachel asked. "Because it's not very funny."

"I'm serious. I've never seen a man more devoted to a woman than Gabriel was to you. Love like that doesn't die. I'm sure both of you still have feelings for each other. Spending time in each other's presence can spark the flame all over again."

"Hush, Mama, before he hears you. I couldn't bear it if Gabriel thinks I'm plotting with you to win him back. It couldn't be any further from the truth. Besides, do you honestly think he wants anything to do with me after what I put him through?" She wasn't sure if it was Helene's illness talking, but Rachel had to set her straight before her mother dug in her heels. Helene Marshall was a force to be reckoned with when she fixed her mind on something.

The older woman's jaw trembled. "Those girls deserve a family. And you shouldn't walk through life alone."

Rachel saw the raw emotion etched on Helene's face and she knew it was genuine.

Although she'd gone about it the wrong way, Rachel knew instinctively her mother hadn't been trying to hurt her by bringing up Jonathan in front of Gabriel. In her own way, she'd been coming from a good place, even though it was misguided. The idea of her reuniting with Gabriel after all these years was far-fetched to say the least. She imagined neither one of them was the same person they'd been three years ago. Time hadn't stood still.

She reached out and gripped her mother's hand. "I know you're only trying to help me and the girls, but I don't want you to be disappointed when it doesn't come to pass. He and I have both moved on from our time together. There's way too much water under that particular bridge. I'm not in love with Gabriel anymore. It's possible that I might find happiness with someone in the future and be able to give the girls a father figure, but it won't be with Gabriel. Not now. Not ever."

A sound in the doorway drew her attention. Gabriel was standing there with his tool belt slung around his shoulder. Rachel knew immediately he had overheard everything she'd just said about him. Her heart ached with regret. He had no way of knowing she'd only responded in that particular way because Helene had been matchmaking. Before she could say a word, Gabriel said, "I just wanted to say goodbye. I need to make another trip to the hardware store. I'll be back at the end of the week when I get back from my trip to Lake Hood." With a terse nod, he was gone.

"I think he heard you," Helene chided, shaking her head ruefully and letting out a tutting sound.

Rachel let out a groan. It was just like her mother to stir the pot then place the blame elsewhere. She really didn't want Gabriel to leave with those being the last words he heard from her lips.

"I'll be right back." She needed to catch up with him before he left. There were a few things she needed to get straight with him and there was no time like the present.

Gabriel couldn't have walked any faster even if his feet were on fire.

So much for him believing he could be in Rachel's presence without any issues cropping up. He felt as if he'd just walked a mile over hot coals with no shoes on. The tension in the Marshall household had been off the charts. All he wanted to do at the moment was head back to his house and hang out with Scooby, his Siberian husky. Dogs were the most loyal creatures on earth, only asking to love and be loved. It was a shame people couldn't be more like canines.

"Gabriel! Wait." Rachel's voice called out after him. He turned around to see her standing in the doorway. She stepped out onto the porch, closing the door behind her.

"You really shouldn't come outside with only a sweater on. It's pretty cold out here," he said, his gaze skimming over her winter sweater and jeans.

"I won't keep you. I just wanted to apologize." She wrapped her arms around her middle.

"For what?" he asked, hoping she wasn't going to bring up the conversation he'd just overheard. He didn't need her trying to make amends for what they both already knew. She'd long ago decided he wasn't going to play a part in her future.

"I'm sorry you got embroiled in that discussion about Lizzy and Faith's father. It wasn't fair to you. I could see it made you uncomfortable."

"No worries, Rachel. I'm a big boy." He gritted his teeth. "For the record, I think your ex is a colossal jerk. Any man who walks away from his responsibilities is no man at all."

She wrinkled her nose. "That's a pretty accurate description of him. Frankly, he's the one who's the big loser in all of this. He'll never know how wonderful Lizzy and Faith are. He's missing out on something pretty spectacular. God's greatest gift. He blessed me twice over with the girls." Rachel smiled at him.

Gabriel grinned back at her. "I'm happy you have the girls. They certainly are blessings."

"Thank you. By the way, what you just overheard me saying to my mother—"

He held up his hands. "It's all right, Rachel. We've been done for a long time now. You didn't say anything I didn't already know. I'm glad you came back to take care of your mother. She needs you."

"Me too. Even though things between us have always been a bit strained, I want to be with her for the time she has left. I want my girls to get to know her before she leaves us."

Gabriel frowned. "Rachel. Helene may be struggling with a breast cancer diagnosis, but she does have options. If she would agree to undergo any of the treatments, the doctor assured her she would have a decent chance to beat this cancer."

Rachel's eyes widened, and a look of confusion passed over her face.

"W-what are you saying? She never mentioned any possible treatments."

Rachel's shock was on full display. Clearly, Helene hadn't been honest with her daughter about her situation. Gabriel couldn't help but feel sorry for Rachel, and he reminded himself to be patient. Rachel had already lost one parent. He imagined the idea of her mother being so ill must be extremely difficult to bear.

"Helene might have a shot at getting better if she'll agree to some of the procedures. Up until now she's refused to have any surgery. Of all the people in the world, you're probably the only one who can convince her to give it a shot."

"Me? But she didn't even tell me she had any other options. She made it sound like things were out of her control. I have no idea why she would hide things from me. I'm an RN. Didn't she think I could handle it?" Her voice was full of confusion and hurt.

"Talk to her. Get her to open up to you. Having you

and the girls here might just be the motivation she needs to push herself to get better. I think she's afraid."

"Mama? Afraid?" She scoffed. "That doesn't sound like her. The woman is made of steel."

Gabriel made a face. "Not really, Rachel. She has cracks just like the rest of us. She's very vulnerable right now due to her illness. I can see a big difference in her since your arrival. She's more like her old self. Sharper. Livelier. I think she's more joyful."

"Oh, thank you for telling me. It means the world to me," Rachel said, quickly erasing the distance between them before throwing herself against his chest and wrapping her arms around him.

The unexpected gesture completely caught him off guard. One moment she was standing in front of him and the next she was in his arms. He felt his shoulders stiffen. A light floral scent filled his nostrils, reminding him of a hundred nights he'd held her in his arms as they watched the northern lights shimmering in the heavens. Raw emotions swept over him, catapulting him straight into the past. Coming to his senses, Gabriel abruptly pulled away from their embrace. This was the last thing he needed in his life. He wasn't going to allow himself to get swept up again by Rachel. She'd given him enough heartache to last a lifetime. Never again!

He took a step away from her, drawing in a steadying breath. "You're welcome. I really need to go run this errand so I can get home to Scooby." Without waiting for a reply, he turned away from Rachel and began heading toward his vehicle with fast strides.

His breathing was labored and his palms were sweaty

as he settled himself behind the wheel of his truck. Having Rachel in his arms was far too dangerous to his equilibrium. As it was, he had to keep reminding himself of all the ways she'd shattered him into a million pieces. And he still wasn't whole. Yet every moment spent in her presence highlighted all of the reasons why he'd once loved her.

What he needed to do was remember the dark weeks and months he'd gone through after her desertion. During that miserable time, it had hurt to even take a deep breath. He'd barely slept or eaten. Gabriel had transformed into a shell of his former self. He'd given up on life and love.

As a result, he'd vowed never to allow love to blindside him ever again.

Chapter Five

Rachel maneuvered the back roads leading to the center of town like a pro. She felt very confident behind the wheel, which wasn't always the case on snowy Alaskan terrain. Learning how to drive over these snow-packed roads as a teenager had been a rite of passage. She smiled as she remembered how her teddy bear of a father cringed every time she hit the gas during their driving lessons. The look etched on his face had been one of pure terror. Just the thought of it made her chuckle out loud.

It was nice to finally be able to think of him without feeling as if she couldn't breathe.

They had made so many beautiful memories together. Instead of dwelling on his last moments, Rachel wanted to honor the way he'd lived his life. She'd tried very hard over the past few years to make progress toward that goal. Her therapist had been very encouraging about the strides she'd made toward healing, although she knew she still had a long way to go on her journey.

As she drove past familiar sights, Rachel felt a hitch in her heart upon seeing her father's old hangar. One of these days she would summon the courage to stop by with the twins for a visit, but not today. She wasn't ready for such an emotional trip down memory lane.

Thoughts of Gabriel popped into her mind. The last time she'd seen him he'd been trying to place some distance between them by pushing her away from him. His actions had been symbolic, she realized. Although it had hurt to be rejected by Gabriel, she really couldn't blame him. Why would he want to have her in his arms after everything she'd put him through? She wondered if he'd returned from his trip to Lake Hood. It was a flight he'd made dozens of times and thankfully it wasn't one of the riskier ones. Her own father had flown to the seaplane base on many occasions during his career. A few times he'd taken Rachel along with him, and on those occasions she'd been on top of the world. Daddy's little girl. He'd always made her feel special. And so very loved.

She looked in her rearview mirror just as Lizzy reached out to hold hands with her twin sister. Faith let out a sharp cry when her fingers ended up in her sister's mouth. "No, Lizzy. Be nice. Don't give Faith a boo-boo. You're making her sad." A contrite Lizzy began placing kisses on Faith's hand, and within seconds, the tears subsided. Lizzy was teething something fierce and didn't hesitate to clamp down on anything in her eyesight. Taking the girls into town with her was an act born out of necessity. She couldn't very well leave them at the house with her ailing mother.

A few days ago she'd had the opportunity to meet

Tessa Jacobsen, the nurse who'd been coming to the house to help out with her mother's care. She was a wonderful woman who had an easy manner and a generous heart. Dedicated and hardworking, she got along famously with Helene. Having Tessa's assistance on a part-time basis would help Rachel out tremendously. Neil offered to pay for Tessa's services, which was a huge relief. As it was, Rachel needed a mother's helper to assist her in watching the girls for a few hours in the afternoon so she could focus on Helene's care. One-year-olds tended to need a lot of attention. She'd been juggling those responsibilities along with her mother's care since her arrival in Owl Creek and it was getting a bit complicated, not to mention exhausting. Spending one-on-one time with her mother was crucial, especially in light of her revealing conversation with Gabriel.

She needed Helene to open up to her so she could encourage her to undergo whatever treatments her doctors advised. Although she had an idea of what her mother was facing, Rachel needed to hear it from Helene's lips. Learning she might have a fighting chance had left Rachel feeling hopeful even though broaching the subject was a bit daunting.

While Tessa was on the clock, Rachel decided to drive into town so she could put up a few notices about a babysitter for the girls. Hiring a sitter would free up some of her time so she wasn't constantly feeling torn between the girls and caring for her mother.

Rachel bit her lip as she gazed over at the Snowy Owl diner. It would be the perfect spot to hang up some signs in her search for a mother's helper. Bringing her daughters with her was a bit nerve-racking, since it was the first time she'd ventured into town with them. She knew it was silly to feel as if she owed the towns-folk an explanation for her life choices since she'd left Owl Creek.

No matter what anyone else thought, Lizzy and Faith were her anchors. She couldn't imagine her life without them. It was uncanny how much the twins had trans-formed her world.

"You've got this," she murmured, giving herself a pep talk. If she had a dollar for every time she'd given herself one since the birth of her girls, she would be on easy street. She parked her vehicle, then plucked the girls out of their car seats, placing them side by side in their double stroller. Thankfully the diner had a ramp in addition to the steps. As she propped the door open so she could wheel the stroller inside, a whiff of down-home cooking reached her nostrils.

She wasn't certain if her mind was playing tricks on her, but it seemed as if all eyes were trained on her as she entered Piper's establishment. Bracing herself for whispers or rude stares, Rachel vowed to herself that no matter what, she wasn't going to allow it to break her. Hopefully, they would show her grace.

A few people called out to her while others greeted her with warm smiles. Mrs. Jenkins, her high school English teacher, grabbed her gently by the arm as she passed by her table and said, "It's wonderful to see you back in town. You were always my best student, bar none." A sense of incredible relief spread through her upon hearing her warmhearted words. The looks sent in her direction were filled with curiosity, which was perfectly understandable. She didn't detect a hint of censure in any of their gazes.

As soon as she spotted Rachel, Piper made a beeline in her direction, letting out a delighted squeal as she reached her side. She hugged Rachel before turning her attention to the twins. "I'm so glad you stopped by with your girls. I've been hoping to meet them."

Piper got down on her haunches so she was eye level with Faith and Lizzy. She reached out and gently caressed their faces, one at a time. "Aren't you two just the spitting images of your mama? You're blessed," she said, looking up at Rachel with tears in her eyes. "You always did want to be a mom more than anything else in the world."

Piper's words served as a reminder of her younger self. Back then Rachel dreamed of marrying Gabriel and creating a family with him while juggling a nursing career. Her life had seemed perfect until she'd scratched the surface and discovered flaws.

"Don't look now but your ex-fiancé is here," Piper murmured in a low voice.

Rachel turned around and scanned the area, immediately spotting Gabriel sitting by himself at a booth. They made eye contact and she responded to his nod with a wave before turning back around. She felt a profound sense of relief simply knowing he was back safe and sound from his trip to Lake Hood. His well-being was no longer her concern, but she couldn't deny she still cared.

"I said not to look!" Piper said in a loud whisper, rolling her eyes.

Rachel covered her face with her hand and let out a nervous laugh. The sight of Gabriel was causing a funny, fluttering sensation in her stomach. It was an odd feeling to realize he still had such a strong effect on her. Her ex, Jonathan, had never made her feel anything remotely like this. Seeing him seated at that particular booth brought to mind all the times they'd shared a meal at this very diner. Back when Piper's dad, Jack, had been alive he'd always made a point to treat them to ice cream sundaes after their meal. She knew Piper, Hank and their mother, Trudy Miller, were still mourning their loss. Rachel could empathize with them. Memories of her own father were everywhere in Owl Creek.

Piper let out a groan. "Do you remember Shelby Warren?"

"Of course I do. She has the distinction of being the snarkiest person I've ever had the misfortune to meet."

Piper made a face. "I'm so sorry, but she's coming straight toward us."

The strong odor of cloying perfume announced the arrival of Shelby, one of Rachel's former classmates. With her long dark hair and wide-set eyes, she was a very attractive woman. Rachel had always thought it was a shame that her beauty only rested on the surface.

"Well, I almost can't believe my eyes," Shelby said, her tone full of surprise. "Rachel Marshall! I never thought I'd see you back in Owl Creek, especially not after the way you left Gabriel in the lurch." The smirk on the woman's face was a familiar one. Shelby had been Rachel's nemesis all through school. She'd had a major crush on Gabriel, and as a result, had taken out all her animosity on Rachel.

Shelby smiled in the direction of Lizzy and Faith. "They're such cute girls, Rachel. Congratulations. Is your husband here with you?" Shelby made a point to dramatically look down at Rachel's naked ring finger.

"No, he's not," Rachel replied smoothly. She didn't owe Shelby any explanations about her marital status or lack thereof. She had a good idea her former classmate knew she was an unwed mother since gossip tended to fly on the wind in Owl Creek. In the past Rachel had always taken the high road with Shelby, but she wasn't about to allow her to walk all over her. She'd become a stronger person over the past few years thanks to everything she'd been through.

"Speaking of husbands, how's Earl?" Piper asked, her expression deadpan.

Shelby bristled. "I think you know we're not together anymore, Piper!" With a toss of her long mane of hair, Shelby turned on her heel and flounced back to her table.

Piper covered a smirk with her hand. "That was bad of me, wasn't it?"

"Frankly, I'm just grateful she's not standing here grilling me anymore," Rachel said with a sigh. "When I think of all the ways she tried to put me down in high school it gives me the shivers. I wish I'd had the strength to stand up to her."

Piper reached out and squeezed her hand. "You've grown a lot since that time. I can tell just by looking at you and the way you carry yourself that you're different than the woman who fled rather than marry the most perfect bachelor in town." She wagged her eyebrows at Rachel. "Some wild theories have been tossed around about why you ran off, Rachel. I'd still like to hear the truth from your lips if you want to share it with me."

"I appreciate the fact that you've noticed those changes. They haven't come easily." Rachel reached down and ran her fingers through Faith's curls. "I can't take all the credit though. Being a mother has given my life a newfound purpose. And I would love to explain it all to you when we have some private time together."

"Why don't you grab a quick bite to eat while you're here? I'm a pro at creating menu items for one-year-olds thanks to my niece Addie. I make the best homemade chicken nuggets." She winked at Rachel. "They're a real crowd-pleaser for the toddler set."

Apparently, Hank had a little girl around the same age as her own. Due to her friendship with Beulah, she'd known about Hank's upcoming wedding to Sage, the long-lost North family member. She'd also told Rachel all about Hank being a single dad to Addie. Beulah had been a great source of information during the time Rachel had been away from Owl Creek.

"Food sounds tempting right about now, but I really should hang up this help wanted notice. I'd planned to walk down Main Street and put up my other ads. I really need a part-time sitter who can help me with the twins. There are going to be times when Mama needs my undivided attention," she explained. "I don't want to let her down."

"I'll make sure I spread the word." The grumbling of Rachel's stomach drew a grin from Piper. "Seems like your stomach agrees with me. I can whip something up really fast for you. It's lunchtime and you guys need to eat something, especially if you're going to go venturing all over town."

Rachel couldn't resist the lure of food. She'd foolishly skipped breakfast and her stomach was protesting that decision. With a nod, she gave in. "I suppose we can stay for a little bit."

With Piper's help, Rachel settled the girls into high chairs and ordered a small meal for the three of them. After her friend dashed off to put their orders in, Rachel reached into her diaper bag and took out a plastic bag filled with Goldfish. She poured a handful onto the table in front of them in order to tide them over until their lunches arrived. Over the past six months she'd gotten used to bringing a little snack wherever they went. It kept the girls occupied and staved off hunger.

A short while later Piper returned with the food and placed their orders down in front of them. "Here you go, ladies. Enjoy!"

"Thank you for being so thoughtful," Rachel said, quickly noticing how Piper had cut up the chicken into small pieces perfect for toddlers.

Piper winked at her. "It's my pleasure. I'm just so thrilled to have you back in town along with your girls."

"Thanks. Even though we came back for Mama, I'm excited about being here for the holidays. Jack would be so proud of you, Piper, for carrying on his legacy. The place looks amazing."

Piper's warm brown skin seemed to lose a few shades. Her lips began to tremble uncontrollably. She let out an anguished sound, raising her hand to cover her mouth. Tears pooled in her eyes.

"What's wrong?" Rachel asked, standing up to place a comforting arm around her. "Did I say something to upset you?"

Piper shook her off. "I—I'm sorry. I can't talk about this right now," she said before turning around and beating a fast path toward the kitchen. Before Rachel could respond, she'd disappeared, leaving her to question her next move. She couldn't very well follow after Piper and leave her girls all by themselves at the table. Just as she sank back down into her seat, Gabriel appeared at the table, his handsome face creased with worry.

"Is everything all right?" he asked. "I couldn't help but notice what just happened with Piper."

She shook her head, feeling confused by Piper's distress. "I'm not sure, to be honest. She ran off without telling me what's going on." Rachel felt powerless. She'd just repaired her friendship with Piper and yet she had no clue as to what had led her to become so distraught. Once they had known each other so well Piper would have confided in her on the spot.

Gabriel frowned. "She's been really emotional lately. Maybe you should go check on her."

"I was thinking the same thing, but I just don't want to make matters worse."

Gabriel ran his hand over his jaw. "You're probably one of the only people she'll confide in. I could call

Hank over from the sheriff's office, but he'd probably come in like a cyclone."

Gabriel was right. Hank was a wonderful person, but he'd always been overprotective of his sister. Rachel looked over at her babies. "I would go after her, but I can't leave them alone."

Gabriel darted a glance in the twins' direction. At the moment they were cooing at each other and happily munching on their finger food. They couldn't look more content, although Rachel knew from experience that their moods could change on a moment's notice.

"I—I suppose I could watch them for a few minutes," he said, in an uncertain tone.

Rachel narrowed her gaze as she studied him. "Really? Are you sure? They can be a handful."

"Of course I'm sure. I'm going to be an uncle soon so I need the practice." She watched as he fidgeted with his collar. "They seem pretty happy at the moment. How hard can it be?"

"Famous last words," Rachel murmured as she got up from her seat and headed off in pursuit of Piper.

Two pairs of eyes trailed after Rachel as she walked away from the table. Within seconds their eyes welled up with tears, then their little bow-shaped lips began to tremble. Before he knew it, both were bawling their eyes out. His heart was beating a mile a minute. One moment he'd been eating a bowl of fish chowder with rosemary French fries and the next he was dealing with two one-year-olds simultaneously crying. And he was clueless as to how to stop it.

Gabriel didn't know how he'd ended up minding Rachel's children. He wasn't sure what exactly had gotten into him when he'd made the offer. Connor and Hank would tease him about his nice-guy tendencies. What he knew about babies could easily fit on a postage stamp. He'd been around Hank's daughter Addie on numerous occasions, but he hadn't ever babysat her or changed a diaper. *Oh no!* A feeling of dread washed over him. Surely he wasn't expected to change any diapers. That was well beyond his capabilities.

"Okay, Faith. Lizzy. Mommy will be right back," he said in a cheery voice.

Wait. Which one was Faith, and which one was Lizzy? They were identical even though Rachel had dressed them in distinctly different outfits. One was decked out in baby blue while the other wore red and white. He didn't know how Rachel was able to instantly tell them apart. He supposed it was tied up in motherhood and the endless days and nights she'd spent caring for them.

At the sound of his voice, they both stopped wailing and focused on him with frowns on their faces. Phew. At least they had both stopped crying. He let out a deep breath. Maybe he could pull this off after all.

His peace lasted all of ten seconds until they began sobbing again. The cries were drawing curious stares from the townsfolk.

Gabriel looked around for anything in sight to entertain the girls. A diaper bag sat on the booth seat where Rachel had been sitting. He reached for it and went through the contents. One small, funny-looking teddy bear. A rattle. A bunch of diapers. A plastic bag filled with Goldfish. Gabriel remembered the girls happily feeding each other Cheerios at Helene's house. Their plates were now empty. Maybe they were still hungry. He opened up the bag of treats and placed a handful on each of their plates. Suddenly, they were gurgling with laughter and grinning at him as they began eating the snack. A feeling of triumph swept over him. One moment he'd been on the ropes and the next he felt so victorious he wanted to raise his fist in the air.

"What's going on over here? I heard the racket when I walked in. I didn't realize you were taking on babysitting gigs." Connor was standing by the table with his arms folded across his chest. A big grin was etched on his face. "From the looks of it, you're a natural."

"I'm just helping out in a crunch," he said, feeling sheepish. His gaze wandered back to the girls. They were pretty adorable with their infectious grins and the happy noises they were making.

Connor's face fell. "Wait a minute. Are these Rachel's girls?" he asked, a deep frown marring his brow.

"Yes," he admitted, bracing himself for his pal's reaction. "And before you lecture me about being a pushover, I consider it simply being a good guy in a moment of need."

Connor sucked his teeth. "What are you doing, Gabe? After everything she did to you, you're still allowing her to walk all over you. Why would you even want to do her a favor? It's opening a door that should be firmly closed."

Gabriel bristled. He hated how being a generous person always resulted in his being called a softy. His faith had taught him to give of himself without reservation. He didn't know how to be any other way. Rachel had wronged him in the past, but it wasn't a reason not to grant her a simple favor, especially when it benefited Piper, as well.

"You don't know what you're talking about!" he said through clenched teeth. "She doesn't have that power over me any longer. This is simply a good deed. End of story."

Connor leaned over so he was eye to eye with Gabriel. He spoke in a low tone. "Whether you realize it or not, you're in danger of getting tangled up with her all over again. If you're not careful, you're going to find yourself right back where you were three years ago. That's not a place anyone who cares about you wants to see you in."

With a shake of his head, Connor strode away from the table and headed over to the pick-up counter. Gabriel chewed on his lip as he replenished the Goldfish on the girls' plates. Whether he wanted to admit it to himself or not, he was forced to consider Connor's dire warning. The last thing he wanted was to relive his painful past with Rachel.

He'd barely made it through in one piece the last time.

Rachel knocked gently on the office door in the rear of the kitchen. She slowly turned the knob and entered, even though she hadn't heard Piper telling her to come in. Her heart dropped the moment she saw her friend sitting at the desk with her head bowed, shoulders heaving with silent cries.

Rachel rushed to her side. "Piper, I just need to know that you're all right. I'm here for you. I'm so sorry if I said something to upset you."

Piper slowly raised her head up. Her eyes were red rimmed and slightly puffy. Rachel knew instinctively this was no simple matter. Her friend wasn't the type of person who was easily reduced to tears.

"It's not your fault. The truth is, things aren't going well with the Snowy Owl." She began sniffling to stem the tide of tears. "If I don't come up with ways to increase revenue, I might be forced to close the place."

Rachel let out a gasp. She knew all too well what the Snowy Owl meant to Piper. It had been her father's pride and joy. He'd worked endless hours to make the diner a huge success in the community. How in the world had things gone downhill so quickly over the past few years?

"What happened? I always thought the business was solid."

"That's what I believed too," Piper said, her breathing becoming more labored. Her face crumpled again and more tears began to leak from her eyes. "After I began running the place I dug into the books and spotted a few red flags. When I crunched the numbers it became obvious to me that my father overextended himself financially. It was pretty shocking to realize I was facing an uphill battle with the business. There was always something I needed to fix around here and bills to pay. Daddy must've been overwhelmed, and he let things go by the wayside."

She let out a ragged sigh. "Long story short, this

place is bleeding money and I'm running low on hope that things will turn around. This place isn't pulling in customers the way we used to. With new restaurants popping up on Main Street, the competition for business is fierce and it's affecting my bottom line."

"Oh, Piper, I wish there was some way I could help, but I don't have much in the way of savings. I'm just hoping the little I do have will tide us over while we're in town," she said regretfully. Oh how she wished she had a large sum of money to give her dear friend. Watching Piper suffer like this was pure torture.

Piper reached out to pat her hand. "You have Faith and Lizzy to worry about. I would never accept a dime from you, but I will take your prayers."

"I'll be offering those up in abundance. I'm here for you, my friend. Always."

Piper sent her a weak smile that didn't quite make it to her eyes. Rachel knew her friend was hurting in the worst way. Letting go of the diner would be like losing her father all over again. Jack Miller's snowmobile accident had been just as shocking and life altering as the loss of her own father in the plane crash. The two men had each died in the pursuit of an activity they loved, which hadn't made the tragedies any easier to bear. When she'd inherited the diner, Piper had told everyone who would listen that it was her way of honoring Jack. Without the Snowy Owl, she wasn't certain how Piper would cope.

As she sat with Piper and tightly held her hand, Rachel was hit hard with the realization of how much she'd missed out on over the past three years. It hurt to know she hadn't been around when her best friend needed her the most. It made her heart ache to think about how much her mother had suffered dealing with her illness all by herself. Rachel could have done so much to help the ones she loved, if only she'd had the courage to face her fears head on and be honest and open with Gabriel. She sucked in a steadying breath. There was no way to turn back time and change the things she'd done. All Rachel could do now was try to move forward and continue to make amends to all the people she'd hurt by leaving Owl Creek.

Chapter Six

By the time Rachel returned to the table, Faith and Lizzy were getting a bit restless.

Gabriel heaved a tremendous sigh of relief. He hadn't been too confident in his ability to keep the girls entertained much longer. For the last few minutes he'd been making funny faces and playing peekaboo to make the girls giggle. Upon seeing their mother, they both began calling out to her with outstretched hands. The sound of the girls saying Mama tugged at a tender place inside him. There was so much love between these three. It was priceless.

"Is everything all right with Piper?" he asked. It was far better to focus on the matter at hand rather than get caught up in sentimentality.

"She's feeling a little better now." Rachel's features were creased with tension, letting him know she was still worried about her friend.

Gabriel shot her a questioning look. "I don't want to pry, but is it something I can help with?"

"I think she just needs to figure some things out regarding the diner."

"I'm happy she has you to confide in. She works so hard. I'm not sure she's taking enough time for herself. Her entire world seems to revolve around this place."

"Inheriting the diner was a blessing, but it placed a heavy weight on her shoulders. I'm not sure I really helped the situation, but sometimes a listening ear is worth its weight in gold. She knows I'm only a phone call away if she needs me."

He bit his tongue. He really wanted to tell Rachel not to leave Piper in the lurch again, but he knew his words would be laced with a trace of bitterness. There would be no point in fanning the flames.

"I should get going. I still need to hang these flyers up on Main Street. I'm looking for a mother's helper." She gave her watch a quick glance. "I need to make sure I'm back at the house before the visiting nurse leaves so I can talk to her. I have about an hour." Rachel busied herself unfolding the stroller, then placing the girls inside one by one.

"I'm on my way out, as well. Let me help you with the stroller."

"I think I'm good," she said. "I'm so grateful for the ramp outside. It makes life a lot easier."

"At least let me get the door for you," Gabriel offered, walking ahead of Rachel so he could hold the door open for her. He tried to ignore the curious gazes watching their every move. He wouldn't be at all surprised if a rumor about him and Rachel being an item again started to circulate in town. The very thought of it irritated him. He didn't relish the idea of being the subject of town gossip.

Once they were outside and had made their way down the ramp, Rachel turned toward him. With her white knit hat framing her heart-shaped face, she looked so striking he couldn't take his eyes off her. There wasn't a single time he'd ever looked at her and thought anything else. He didn't imagine he ever would. The sight of her always made him pause for a second to catch his breath.

"Thanks for watching the girls. I'm impressed you kept them occupied for all that time."

Her lips twitched with merriment.

"What can I say?" Gabriel teased. "I'm a natural-born baby whisperer. Which way are you headed?"

Rachel pointed down the street to the left. "I was going to pop into the pottery place, then hit the book-store. Hopefully it won't be a problem to hang up my flyers."

"I'm sure no one will give you a hard time. Don't forget about Tea Time. It's really become a popular venue in town. According to my mother, business is really booming."

Rachel winced. Watching her expression, Gabriel had the distinct impression she was uncomfortable at the mention of his mother. Perhaps Rachel was ner-vous about seeing Iris after so many years. The last time they'd seen each other Iris had been knee-deep in wedding plans. It had to be awkward to face some-one you'd wronged so badly. The ripples from Rachel's vanishing act had been widespread. He hadn't been the only person she'd inflicted pain on.

"Did you get an opportunity to talk to Helene yet about what we discussed?" he asked, wanting to steer the subject away from her stopping in at Tea Time.

She looked a bit sheepish. "No, I haven't found the right time to bring it up yet."

"The right time?" he asked, wrinkling his nose. "I don't think you can afford to wait much longer."

"I'll do it soon, Gabriel. It's a bit complicated. I don't want any tension between us," Rachel explained. "You know how Mama can be."

He knew all too well how things could digress between them, but he also knew that Rachel would kick herself later for dragging her feet.

"It probably isn't any of my business, but waiting is problematic. I know it's overwhelming, but you can't run away from this."

She sucked in a shocked breath. "Like I ran away from Owl Creek? Isn't that what you really want to say?" Her question crackled in the air between them.

"It's a fair question, don't you think?" Gabriel snapped, instantly wanting to take back his sharp tone when he saw Rachel's reaction. He didn't know why he'd said it. The words slipped past his lips before he could rein them back in.

Rachel's eyes widened and her nostrils flared as if she'd smelled something rotten.

"Don't worry about my mother," she said curtly. "She's not your concern, Gabriel. And regardless of what you think of me, I have no intention of bailing on her."

She turned on her booted heel and began walking away from him, pushing the stroller at a fast clip. He opened his mouth to call her back, but quickly closed it. He didn't even know what to say. How had things spiraled so quickly out of control between them?

He stood for a moment and watched Rachel until she disappeared through the doors of Clay with Me, the pottery store. A part of him wondered if he'd intended to pick at Rachel with his comment. It made him feel ashamed of himself. Despite his desire to put everything behind him, there was still something simmering just below the surface that rose up without warning at times like this. It was like a wound that hadn't healed and continued to ache.

Perhaps he'd been kidding himself to think he could maintain a cordial relationship with Rachel with no complications. The past kept rising up to remind him of his hurts.

By the time she reached the North Star chocolate shop to drop off her flyers, Rachel felt as if her head might explode. How foolish she'd been to think she and Gabriel could get along so harmoniously with so much standing between them. It had only been a matter of time before harsh words were spoken. It annoyed her to no end that Gabriel seemed to be judging her based on the past.

She was muttering to herself as she entered the chocolate shop. The heady smell of sweets filled the air, serving as an immediate mood lifter. She paused for a moment to inhale the tantalizing aroma.

"Rachel! Come on in from the cold! You're a sight for sore eyes." Beulah, dressed in an elegant cream-colored sweater and matching slacks greeted her with enthusiasm. She was wearing her signature strand of pearls around her neck. Rachel couldn't recall ever seeing her without them.

"Hi! I didn't expect to see you here. I thought you would be over at the chocolate factory." As matriarch of the North family, Beulah was involved in all aspects of the running of the family's chocolate company. Primarily, she worked at the production site which was down the street.

"I swing by the shop a few days a week just to check in. It's a nice change of pace," she said with a grin. "Are you in the mood for chocolate?" she asked, pointing to the counter where an assortment of chocolates was on display behind the glass. Rachel felt her mouth watering at the sight of white, milk and dark chocolates. Pecan clusters. Bonbons. Truffles. Nonpareils. Everything a chocoholic could ever want or need.

"I'll never say no to chocolate," she replied, trying to sound cheerful, "but I actually came by to see if I could hang up an advertisement on your community board. I'm in need of someone to help watch the girls part-time."

"Of course you can, Rachel. We get a lot of foot traffic in here and I actually know a few people who might be interested. Lots of folks want to supplement their income." She reached out and tweaked Rachel's chin.

"What's wrong, my dear? You don't look very happy. Is it your mother? I know it must be tough seeing her so unwell. Being a caregiver isn't easy."

She shook her head. "It's not Mama. I just had cross words with Gabriel. One minute he's full of charm and grace, then the next he's like a snapping turtle."

Beulah made a clucking sound. "I'm sorry to hear that. It certainly doesn't sound like the Gabriel I know and love. He's always been such a sweetheart."

"I know I have a lot to atone for, Beulah. I didn't expect to come back to a town that's forgiven and forgotten. Gabriel most of all. But it's a bit frustrating to feel like I'm always going to be judged by my past."

"Don't be too harsh on Gabriel. When you left Owl Creek he was beside himself. I don't think I've ever seen a person more brokenhearted." She patted Rachel's hand. "I'm not trying to make you feel bad, but he truly suffered. Gabriel has always had a special place in my heart due to his friendship with Connor."

She knew Beulah was right. Gabriel had always been a wonderful human being. Kind, loyal and sweet natured. It wounded her to even think about how he must have felt when she abandoned him on the eve of their wedding. It was understandable that he didn't trust her not to run off again when times became tough. But at the same time, it hurt to know he viewed her in such a negative light.

"I fell in love with Gabriel due to his tender heart. But neither one of us is the same person we used to be. It's clear my actions hardened him in some ways. Despite our past connection, we're dodging all these mine-fields whenever we have a conversation."

"Have you ever told Gabriel why you left?" Beulah asked gently. "Perhaps it might change the dynamic between you."

She let out a huff of air. "No, I haven't. I need to come clean with him."

"He's waited a long time for the truth," Beulah said. "Telling him will set you both free. The two of you deserve nothing less."

"I'm so glad I stopped in. You always have an uplifting word."

Beulah chuckled. "I'm not sure everyone here in town would describe me that way, but I'm grateful for the compliment."

The older woman walked behind the counter, then reached into her purse and pulled out an ecru-colored envelope. She held it out to Rachel. "I've been meaning to send this over to the house. Your mother received her invitation weeks ago, and I would love to have you at Sage and Hank's wedding, as well. I would have included you earlier if I'd known back then you were returning to town."

"Oh, Beulah, that's so kind of you. If I haven't said so before, I'm so thrilled for your family being reunited. God was watching over them all these years."

Tears pooled in Beulah's eyes. "He sure did, Rachel. And He brought Sage all the way back to Owl Creek where she belongs. I hope you can join us in celebrating her big day."

"Honestly, I'm not sure I'll be able to find a sitter for

the girls, but it means so much to me that you thought to include me. Ever since I came back to Owl Creek I've been struggling to find my footing here."

"No matter how you left us, you're still a hometown girl at heart. You belong here, honey. Don't ever forget that. You're part of the fabric of this town."

Rachel reached out and hugged Beulah. Although her friend had a reputation in town for being a tough customer, Rachel knew her as a generous and warmhearted woman who had always looked out for her. It meant the world to her to have allies like Beulah in Owl Creek.

Beulah blinked away tears. "Now, before we both get overwhelmed by sentimentality, why don't you hang up your flyer and pick out some chocolates to bring home with you? I know Helene just adores chocolate-covered almonds."

A few minutes later Rachel left the store with a bag full of confections, two sleeping babies and a warm sensation in her heart. It made her feel overjoyed to know she still belonged here in the town she loved so much. Leaving Owl Creek had been a decision born out of fear and indecision. Truly, she hadn't been rational in her thinking back then. She hadn't realized how much she would miss her hometown and its quiet way of life. She hadn't considered how deeply her heart would ache for Gabriel or how regret over leaving him would plague her for weeks and months afterward. If she was being honest with herself, she still hadn't healed from it.

Now, invigorated by her talk with Beulah, she planned to hang up the rest of her notices and then head home to talk to her mother about seeking medical intervention.

She'd already lost so much in her life. Rachel was committed to doing everything in her power to quell her mother's fears so she could move forward. Faith and Lizzy needed their grandmother to be strong, healthy and living her life to the fullest.

Gabriel was wrong. She had no intention of running away from a single thing here in Owl Creek.

Chapter Seven

Two days passed before Rachel was able to talk with her mother about her options for medical treatment. Both the girls had ear infections and she'd spent the past few days caring for them as well as seeing to Helene's needs. Now, more than ever, she needed a helper. Just this afternoon a local woman referred by Beulah had come to the house to be interviewed for the job. Rachel found Sydney Wilson to be caring, experienced and capable. The twins had bonded with her over their favorite Disney character, Ariel. Beulah provided Sydney with a glowing recommendation and she was available to begin working right away.

She had offered Sydney the job on the spot and she'd happily accepted. Rachel couldn't recall ever being so relieved about a situation. Knowing she wouldn't have to twist herself into a pretzel to satisfy everyone's needs was a wonderful feeling.

With the twins down for a nap, Rachel knew it was the perfect time to bring everything out in the open. Helene was sitting at the dining room table working on an elaborate puzzle. Rachel sat down across from her and reached into the box so she could work alongside Helene. When she was younger, she had regularly worked on puzzles with her mother. It had been their bonding time as mother and daughter. It had evaporated in the aftermath of her father's death as each of the members of their small family sought isolation, trying desperately to make sense of their loss.

"We need to talk, Mama. It's important." Rachel met her gaze across the table. She'd tried to make her voice sound firm and no-nonsense.

"Are the girls all right?" Helene asked, raising her hand to her throat. "I know they haven't been feeling well."

"They're fine and on the mend. They happen to be fast asleep at the moment."

"That's good. You scared me for a moment there."

Rachel found it endearing that her mother feared for the health of her grandbabies when she herself was so ill. In the short period of time they'd been in Alaska, Faith and Lizzy had nestled themselves into Helene's heart. It was a true blessing, knowing that her daughters seemed to bring out the best in their grandmother.

"I'm not going to beat around the bush. Gabriel told me you have options for treatment. You never told me Dr. Norris recommended surgery followed by chemotherapy or radiation. I was under the assumption you didn't have any choices based on the information you gave me." Rachel's throat was tight with emotion. Although she was a medical professional, it was still difficult to broach such a delicate subject with her mother.

"I didn't want to worry you, Rachel. Raising the twins by yourself has been stressful enough for you. It was my burden to bear."

"Mama! The girls and I traveled all this way to see you through this. Don't you think you owe me the truth at the very least?"

Helene placed a puzzle piece down on the table with a thump. "Dr. Norris wants me to have surgery—a lumpectomy followed by some chemotherapy. She said it will give me a fighting chance to beat this thing."

Rachel swallowed. "And you said no?"

Although she was used to medical jargon in her profession as a nurse, it felt different to be discussing it with her mother. It was impossible to stay professional when she was so invested. Why hadn't she known this information? She should have pressed Helene more for answers. She should have demanded to talk to her doctor. To date, Helene had only indicated her cancer had worsened to a critical stage. Rachel had taken her at face value, never imagining she was leaving out crucial details.

"Why, Mama? If you can be helped, why not do it?" Emotion rang out in her voice. She couldn't be calm, cool and collected when her mother's life hung in the balance.

Helene shivered and wrapped her arms around her middle. "Oh, Rachel. It was too overwhelming to deal with all the moving pieces. I'd have to fly to Anchorage for the surgery then stay in the hospital for a few days. I've never been in the hospital for anything other than delivering my babies. The idea of it terrifies me."

"We can figure all of that out. I'll be with you every step of the way."

"No! You have the girls to consider. They need you. And it may not do any good in the long run. There are no guarantees." Helene bowed her head as tears trickled down her face. Rachel got up from her chair and moved to the other side of the table. She bent down and wrapped her arms around her mother, holding her tightly as sobs racked her body.

"You need me too," Rachel whispered. "It's okay to need me. It's my turn to care for you like you watched over me when I was a girl. That's how life works."

"I'm so afraid, Rachel," she cried out. "I haven't been this fearful since I lost your father. I've never been a weak person, so I don't understand why I feel so powerless in the face of all this."

"I understand," she said in a low voice. "Life hands us things we have no control over and it's terrifying. But as a woman of faith you know you're not alone on this journey.

"'Fear thou not; for I am with thee.'" Rachel recited the verse from Isaiah.

"'Be not dismayed; for I am thy God.'" Helene continued the passage.

"I'm here, Mama. I'm right here with you and I'm not going anywhere." Rachel rocked her mother in her arms the same way she might soothe her own babies. She knew what it felt like to be crippled by fear. It had been a huge stumbling block in her own life, and she couldn't judge her mother for allowing it to creep in and mess with her mind. Hadn't she allowed fear to drive her away from Owl Creek and Gabriel?

"It's not that I don't want to get better. I would love to be around so I can rock my grandbabies on my knee. I'm just so frightened of what's to come," Helene confessed, her voice cracking midsentence.

"Let's pray, Mama," she said, grasping her mother's hand and joining it with her own. "I know how prayer comforts you. Let's pray for God to guide you out of this place of fear so you can turn inaction into action. If anyone can turn things around, I know He can."

As they bowed their heads and offered up prayers for Helene to have the strength to face her apprehension, Rachel added in her own silent prayer that she would be able to summon the courage to finally face Gabriel and tell him her truths.

If she was asking her mother to be brave, Rachel knew she could ask no less of herself.

Gabriel stood in front of the Marshalls' house, pausing as he prepared to enter their home so he could continue to work on the playroom. Knowing he couldn't drag his feet any longer, he gently rapped on the door.

Helene had given him a key weeks ago in the event that she couldn't make it to the door and he needed access to the house. She'd encouraged him to use it even if they were at home. Gabriel didn't feel entirely comfortable doing so, especially now that Rachel was residing there. It would be awkward for both of them if he randomly entered the house.

It had been almost a week since he'd seen Rachel and Helene. He hoped things wouldn't be tense between him and Rachel after the harsh words they'd exchanged. Even though he'd tried to keep thoughts of her from creeping into his mind, it had been impossible. She seemed to hover in the air around him even when he was miles and miles away from Owl Creek.

He'd been away from town doing what he loved best of all—flying customers all over Alaska. Although he enjoyed all aspects of being a pilot, he had to admit he truly relished exploring the rugged terrain and the raw, uninhabited places in the Last Frontier. It provided a bit of excitement in his uneventful life.

His clients had been honeymooners who'd wanted to explore the uninhabited areas in Alaska. He'd drawn up an itinerary for them that included remote areas such as Egg Island and Saint Matthew Island. He'd flown through the Merrill Pass and met up with challenging weather that might have led a less experienced pilot into a world of trouble.

It had been an exhilarating feeling, one he couldn't quite put into words. When he was up in the sky everything seemed inconsequential. It all faded away compared to the unimaginable beauty of the Alaskan terrain. Nothing seemed impossible when he was soaring above the clouds. Being up among the clouds was living out his dreams, and if his new venture panned out, he would be taking a huge leap of faith and stretching himself as a businessman.

The door suddenly opened, and Rachel was standing in front of him with one of the girls—Faith he thought, judging by the little dimple on the right side of her mouth. He'd figured out the slight difference between the girls the other day.

"Come on in," Rachel said, her voice not betraying any animosity. It felt warm and cozy inside when he crossed the threshold. He could hear the fire crackling from the living room.

Once he was inside, Faith stretched out her arms to him. As a safety measure, he placed his tool belt in a secure area before lifting her up and placing her gently against his chest.

"Hey there, beautiful. Don't you look pretty today," he told her, enjoying the way she gave him a sweet smile and a giggle in return for his compliment.

"It seems you've made a friend," Rachel said. "She doesn't take to just anybody. You must have made a good impression on her at the diner."

"We bonded, didn't we, Faith?" he asked, seeing the surprised look on Rachel's face when he uttered her daughter's name. He guessed most people couldn't differentiate between the two toddlers.

Gabriel held Faith tightly in his arms, realizing for the first time how sturdy she was despite her tiny stature. She smelled like baby powder and lemons, and her brown curls gently framed her sweet face. Faith grinned up at him, showcasing the beginnings of her two front teeth poking through the gums. His heart lurched. He felt a strong desire to protect this little girl with all of his might. Someone so little and defenseless should always be sheltered from the storms of life. He felt fury all over again that her father had walked out of her life.

"Okay, Faith," Rachel said in a singsong voice, "We need to go sit back down for lunch and let Gabriel have his arms back." Suddenly the little girl wasn't snuggled against him any longer, leaving him feeling a bit empty.

It was a startling realization.

"I've been wanting to apologize to you for what I said the other day." He shook his head ruefully. "I had no right to make that comment to you about running away from things. It wasn't fair and it served no purpose other than to rile you up. I'm sorry."

She nodded. "Apology accepted. I think you hit a raw nerve, but after I cooled down I realized there's bound to be tension between us. We're kind of fumbling around each other trying to coexist in a very small town. It was inevitable we clashed."

"I know you're going through a lot with Helene being so ill, so it wasn't my place to make things harder. That's all I wanted to say."

"I appreciate it," Rachel said, her brown eyes twinkling. "I better get lunch served before I have a revolt on my hands." Right before she turned away, Faith placed her chubby hand to her mouth and proceeded to blow him a kiss. It was the simplest of gestures, but it melted his heart on the spot. After picking up his tool belt, Gabriel beat a fast path down the hall to the area where he'd been working, hoping a change of scenery would cause him to snap out of it. Everything seemed to be tugging at his emotions today.

"Focus on the matter at hand," he said out loud. "Finishing this project will bring Helene joy. You made her a promise," he reminded himself. "She's counting on you." He didn't need to remind himself that the faster he completed the renovations the sooner he would be away from Rachel and her charming toddlers. They were proving to be quite a distraction to his state of mind.

Gabriel attacked the work with a vengeance, only stopping when his drill suddenly quit working. After a few minutes of checking things over, he concluded that the problem rested with his extension cord. He hoped Helene had a replacement. If not, he'd have to head out to the hardware store in town, which would cost him precious time. He walked down the hallway toward the kitchen, and as soon as he reached the entrance, he heard loud noises that resembled crying.

"Has something happened?" he asked, stopping mid-stride. They'd already seen him standing there so it was too late to gracefully retreat. Hopefully he hadn't stepped into another Marshall family squabble. The last one had proven to be incredibly awkward. "I was hoping to borrow an extension cord. Mine isn't working. Should I come back later on?" He shifted from one foot to the other, all the while hoping fervently that nothing disastrous had taken place.

Rachel was crying. Helene was sniffling back tears. Faith and Lizzy were wailing. He was standing in a room full of sobbing females and he didn't have a clue as to what was going on! Was someone hurt? Had they just received some terrible news? He found himself praying fast and furiously.

"No," Helene said with a shake of her head. "Your timing is perfect."

"Something wonderful has happened!" Rachel announced in a trembling voice. "My prayers have been answered. Mama's agreed to undergo the surgery." Her face lit up with a radiant smile.

"That's fantastic!" Gabriel said, moving toward Helene to envelop her in a huge bear hug. A look of relief was etched on her face, as if she had finally let go of a huge burden. Fear wasn't a rational emotion, yet it still held people in its tight grip.

"Now we just have to figure out how to get to Anchorage," Helene said. "That's where they want to do the procedure."

Rachel patted Helene's hand. "We'll figure it out, Mama. Just leave the details to me. That's the easy part," Rachel said, brushing away tears. "Dr. Norris also said I could administer the chemo here if you get a port put in. You won't even have to leave the house."

"Rachel! I'm not sold on the chemo treatment yet. I've decided to have the surgery but I'm in prayer about the rest of it. The surgery might be sufficient to get me on the path to wellness."

Gabriel observed the look of frustration on Rachel's face. He could tell she wanted to challenge Helene but thought better of it. "One step at a time, Mama. We'll deal with that hurdle later on."

Gabriel cleared his throat. "I'd be honored to fly you to Anchorage, Helene, compliments of Lawson Charters. Just tell me when."

"Oh, Gabriel. What a kind offer!" Helene proclaimed, clapping her hands together. "That would be such a Godsend. Thank you for your generosity."

The look of joy etched on Helene's face would be the only thanks he'd ever need.

"It would be my pleasure to take you there," Gabriel said. "Just let me know the details and I'll make it happen." He might have to juggle a few of his charters, but he would do whatever it took to get Helene to Anchorage. With the company growing so fast, he'd been able to hire two part-time pilots to help ease the flight load.

Helene darted a glance in Rachel's direction. "Rachel? Would that be all right with you? I know you don't like to fly in small planes. We can always take the ferry."

As they all knew, the ferry ride to Anchorage was a bit longer than a flight on his seaplane. Not to mention the waters of Kachemak Bay were choppy in November. In his opinion, Helene would be much more comfortable flying with him. He could make sure she was undisturbed and at ease. The decision didn't rest in his hands though. He'd made the offer and now all he could do was wait for Rachel's response.

For a moment Rachel appeared frozen. She bit her lip and looked back and forth between them. Gabriel could almost see the wheels turning in her head. More than anything, he knew she wanted Helene to get the medical help she so desperately needed to prolong her life. But she also feared small planes due to Lance's death. He knew it must be a terrible dilemma for her.

"Of course, it's okay, Mama. If you can face up to surgery, then surely I can fly in Gabriel's plane." Her smile didn't make its way to her eyes. Gabriel sensed she'd only said the words she knew her mother wanted to hear. He wanted to reassure her, but he didn't really think it was his place.

"Praise the Lord," Helene exclaimed. "I just love the way this is all coming together. You can't tell me that the good Lord didn't have His hand in this."

Gabriel nodded in concurrence. "I agree with you. God has plans for you, Helene. And this is the first step on your journey to wellness."

"Oh, Gabriel, you're going to make me tear up again and I've never been a big crier until lately," Helene said, blotting her eyes with a tissue. "I think it has something to do with being a grandmother. It's brought out my soft side."

"We're grateful for your offer, Gabriel. Let me get that extension cord for you," Rachel murmured, disappearing for a moment as she rummaged in the utility closet. She returned with an extension cord in her hands and handed it over to him.

"Thanks. I better get back to work. I have my final tuxedo fitting this afternoon for Sage and Hank's wedding." He felt his grin stretching from ear to ear. "I'm not sure I've ever seen my buddy so thrilled about anything in his life." As one of Hank's closest friends, he could easily vouch for his bliss. But now, his own future stretched out before him like a blank canvas. It was a bit unsettling. It would be exciting if his aviation venture panned out, but he wanted to settle down like his best friend. He didn't want to walk through life alone.

"I'm so excited about the wedding," Helene said in a gushing tone, interrupting his thoughts. "I can't think of the last time I've attended one. It's been years." Her tone was filled with glee. Prior to her illness, Helene had been a bit of a social butterfly, constantly attending town events and celebrations. He considered it a good sign that she was enthused about the upcoming nuptials.

Rather reluctantly, Gabriel met Rachel's gaze. He imagined they were both thinking the very same thing. The last wedding might have been their own if things hadn't gone so far astray. The very thought of it made his stomach hurt.

No matter what he did, all roads seemed to lead back to Rachel and what might have been. It was a frustrating feeling, as if he would never be able to escape their shared past. He let out a sigh of exasperation. Before Rachel's return to Owl Creek he'd convinced himself that he had made great progress, but now, faced with her presence in town, he felt as if he'd been backsliding for weeks.

He ought to keep a clear distance from her so she wouldn't be in his thoughts so much of the time. Gabriel needed to dig down deep and finish this renovation project. Once it was completed, he wouldn't be forced to see her all the time. Perhaps then he would find some measure of peace.

Chapter Eight

"You may now kiss the bride." The church erupted into applause as Hank and Sage followed the pastor's instructions and concluded the wedding ceremony with a romantic, tender kiss. Gabriel found himself cheering louder than anyone. Despite what he'd been through, he still believed in true love. He couldn't think of a couple who deserved it more than these two.

He hadn't known how he would feel standing up for Hank as he married the love of his life in the same church he and Rachel had chosen for their ill-fated wedding. Although he'd felt a bit funny the moment Rachel and Helene had entered the church and taken their seats, he had been able to enjoy all the wonderful aspects of the service. There was something about weddings that made a person believe in love everlasting.

His heart was full of happiness for Hank and Sage. Finding a forever type of love was something to be celebrated, and seeing the devoted couple exchange their vows was an experience he couldn't put into words. It was sacred and awe-inspiring. He was honored to be one of Hank's groomsmen and to be a part of their epic love story.

Life sometimes was stranger than fiction. Sage had hidden her identity as Lily North when she'd come to Owl Creek. By the time the truth was revealed, she and Hank were head over heels in love with one another. There was so much symmetry to Sage returning to the place of her birth and finding her happy ending with a hometown boy.

As everyone began to file out of the church after the bride and groom, he found himself standing in front of the church next to Helene and Rachel. This was the downside of small towns. Even if you were trying to avoid someone, you ended up in their orbit. And he couldn't very well walk past them without speaking.

"You look wonderful, Gabriel," Helene said in a gushing tone.

"Thank you. The two of you look great, as well," he said, his eyes lingering for a few seconds too long on Rachel. In her turquoise dress and with her upswept hairdo, she radiated an air of elegance. As always, she looked stunning.

Rachel appeared to be a bit ill at ease. "It's a little strange not to have the twins with me. I can't remember the last time I went out to a social function."

"It's good for you to do things without your babies," Helene said. "It's not healthy to be with them all the time." Gabriel winced at the woman's harsh tone. He couldn't imagine it had been well received by Rachel, whose lips pursed in response to her mother's scolding.

"One Minute" Survey

You get up to **FOUR books** <u>and</u> Mystery Gifts...

YOU pick your books –
WE pay for everything.
You get up to FOUR new books and TWO Mystery Gifts..
absolutely FREE!
Total retail value: Over $20!

Dear Reader,

Your opinions are important to us. So if you'll participate in our fast
and free "One Minute" Survey, **YOU** can pick up to four wonderful
books that **WE** pay for!

As a leading publisher of women's fiction, we'd love to hear from
you. That's why we promise to reward you for completing our
survey.

IMPORTANT: Please complete the survey and return it. We'll send
your Free Books and Free Mystery Gifts right away. **And we pay
for shipping and handling too!** ← *We pay for EVERYTHING!*

Try **Love Inspired® Romance Larger-Print** books and fall in love
with inspirational romances that take you on an uplifting journey of
faith, forgiveness and hope.

Try **Love Inspired® Suspense Larger-Print** books where courage
and optimism unite in stories of faith and love in the face of danger

Or TRY BOTH!

Thank you again for participating in our "One Minute"
Survey. It really takes just a minute (or less) to complete the
survey… and your free books and gifts will be well worth it!

Sincerely,

Pam Powers

Pam Powers
for Reader Service

"One Minute" Survey

GET YOUR FREE BOOKS AND FREE GIFTS!

✓ Complete this Survey ✓ Return this survey

1 Do you try to find time to read every day?
☐ YES ☐ NO

2 Do you prefer books which reflect Christian values?
☐ YES ☐ NO

3 Do you enjoy having books delivered to your home?
☐ YES ☐ NO

4 Do you find a Larger Print size easier on your eyes?
☐ YES ☐ NO

YES! I have completed the above "One Minute" Survey. Please send me my Free Books and Free Mystery Gifts (worth over $20 retail). I understand that I am under no obligation to buy anything, as explained on the back of this card.

☐ I prefer Love Inspired® Romance Larger Print 122/322 IDL GNTG

☐ I prefer Love Inspired® Suspense Larger Print 107/307 IDL GNTG

☐ I prefer BOTH 122/322 & 107/307 IDL GNTS

FIRST NAME | LAST NAME

ADDRESS

APT.# | CITY

STATE/PROV. | ZIP/POSTAL CODE

Sometimes he wanted to pull Helene aside and tell her to watch her sharp tongue. It had never helped her relationship with Rachel to be so critical. He knew she came from a place of love, but he feared it got lost in translation.

"I see Lincoln is motioning me over," Helene said, her eyes full of mischief. "I better go say hello before he makes a fuss. He's the biggest flirt in Owl Creek." With a dramatic eye roll, she walked away from them to join the elderly widower and his cronies over by the driveway.

"So, who's watching the girls?" he asked Rachel, trying to fill the silence. "Did you manage to find a sitter?"

Her face lit up. "Yes, I did. Beulah found someone who's the perfect fit. Her name is Sydney and the girls have really taken to her. She actually works part-time hours at the chocolate factory."

"Beulah to the rescue," Gabriel said with a chuckle. "Is there anything she can't accomplish? I'm beginning to wonder if she sleeps at night."

"She's incredible. I'm feeling really thankful for all of her help. Sydney is going to be a great asset. Now I'll have more time to help Mama with all of her needs."

"It sounds like everything is falling into place," he said.

"It really is, especially with Mama agreeing to the surgery."

"Gabriel!" The sound of his name being called drew his attention to Connor, who was standing curbside with a mischievous grin on his face. He'd completely forgotten about their plan to decorate Hank's car before he left the church for the reception at the Norths' estate. It seemed as if his pal had started without him.

"It looks like Hank and Sage have a surprise in store for them," Rachel murmured, a smile playing around her lips. He loved watching her in relaxed moments like this when he could almost pretend as if nothing had ever come between them.

"Duty calls. I'm sure our paths will cross at the reception," he said as he moved away from her and navigated his way through the crowd until he reached Connor's side. He didn't have to inquire about the expression stamped on the other man's face.

"You and Rachel are setting tongues wagging," Connor said with a raised brow.

Gabriel held up his hands to ward off a lecture. "We were just talking. There's nothing more to it than being cordial. I wish people would give it a rest."

"All right," Connor said, holding up his hands in defeat. "Don't blame the messenger. I was just giving you a heads-up."

Gabriel muttered to himself. "People here in Owl Creek gossip as much as they breathe."

"No argument there, my friend."

"I can't control what other people say, only what I do. I promise you this. There's nothing going on between Rachel and I. And there never will be." Even as he said the decisive words, he felt a tightening sensation in the middle of his chest. Although he'd tried to sound convincing, he wasn't certain he believed it himself.

Beareth all things, believeth all things, hopeth all things, endureth all things. The verse spoken during the wedding ceremony had brought tears to Rachel's eyes. Seeing Hank and Sage so deeply committed to one another made her feel hopeful and sentimental. Sometimes true love did triumph over adversity. She didn't think it was possible to bear witness to their love and not be incredibly moved by it. The guests had all relocated to the North home after the bride and the groom drove away with cans, streamers and big pink-and-white balloons attached to the back of their truck.

During the ceremony her eyes had locked with Gabriel, who looked spectacular in his dark tuxedo and crisp white shirt. Her mind immediately went to their own wedding that wasn't. She imagined he would have appeared nearly identical dressed in his own groom's tuxedo. Rachel pushed away the thought of Gabriel in his finery. Thinking about it always left her with a feeling of angst coiled in her belly.

She stepped outside to the patio, eager to get away from the crowd for a few minutes. Rachel might just scream if another person asked her about whether she was moving back permanently to town. She'd been dumbfounded when an old classmate had asked her if she and Gabriel were getting back together. It seemed that the townsfolk hadn't given up on them, even if they had been over and done with a long time ago.

The sky was the color of deep pewter, sprinkled with a dazzling array of stars. A pale sliver of moon hung in the night sky. Even though the temperature was frigid, Rachel felt as if she could stay out here for hours simply gazing up at the heavens. When everything was calm and still like this she always felt closer to God. Perhaps if the timing was right, she might catch a glimpse of the northern lights.

"I wish. I wish," she said, pressing her eyes closed and wishing upon a star as she'd done so many times as a child. She'd needed a breath of fresh air to steady herself after soaking in all of the love between the happy couple. The love they shared shimmered and pulsed in the air around them. It had been palpable. Everyone in the church had surely known they were in the presence of love everlasting.

Her chest felt tight and for the life of her she couldn't even identify the emotions roiling around inside her. Could she admit even to herself how she still felt a deep sense of longing for what might have been if she hadn't run away from Gabriel? Something about seeing Sage in her romantic ivory-colored gown had revived all of her own hopes and dreams.

Ever since she was a little girl, Rachel had fantasized about walking down the aisle toward her forever—a husband who would stick by her side no matter what challenges life threw in their direction. That dream hadn't completely died. It still rested inside the deepest part of her, like a precious pearl at the bottom of the ocean.

She had been so close to tying the knot with Gabriel. Their future had been stretched out before them like a glowing beacon. She shut her eyes tightly and shook off the memories of his proposal and the moment he'd placed the antique engagement ring on her finger. There had been no doubt in her mind that they were destined to spend the rest of their lives together.

And yet everything between them had crumbled into nothing because of her fears.

Would she ever find love again? She would give anything to feel that sweeping, soaring feeling pulsing through her veins—the way Gabriel had once made her feel. Jonathan had never made her feel beautiful or loved. She'd been so desperate to feel that way—to experience anything that might make her feel as alive as she'd felt when she'd been with Gabriel—that she had plunged into an unhealthy relationship. It had been far from loving, but in the end, it had given her Lizzy and Faith—the true joys of her life.

The sound of footsteps jolted her out of her thoughts. She knew before she turned around it was Gabriel standing behind her. It was as if the atmosphere around her hummed with his energy. She could smell the sandalwood scent that hovered around him.

"What are you doing out here?" he asked. "You're going to get hypothermia if you're not careful. That shawl you're wearing can't be keeping you very warm."

Rachel wrapped her arms around her middle, turning her head so their gazes met. Being so close to him while he was wearing his midnight-colored tuxedo and looking more handsome than a man had a right to look only served as a distraction. No wonder her thoughts had veered toward their shared past. It seemed as if he was in the very air she breathed in Owl Creek. Every time he was in her orbit, she felt her pulse skitter with awareness. This moment was no exception. She was acutely aware of his rugged presence and the way her heart tended to beat a little bit faster whenever he was nearby. It confused and startled her to feel so much for someone who was rooted so firmly in her past.

"I only came out here for a minute," she answered. "It doesn't seem possible, but I'd almost forgotten how stunning an Alaskan sky can be." She lifted her face upward, her gaze fixed on the crescent moon. It almost appeared as if she could reach out and touch it.

When she turned back toward Gabriel he was shrugging off his tuxedo jacket. He gently placed it over her shoulders. "You must have forgotten you're not in Denver anymore. It doesn't take long to freeze."

"Now you're going to be cold," she said, letting out a sound of protest.

"I'm good. I've got long sleeves and a vest," he murmured. "Plus I worked up a sweat dancing with Beulah. She puts me to shame," he said, chuckling.

"Always the gentleman," Rachel said as a feeling of warmth washed over her. She had no idea whether it was Gabriel's jacket or his mere presence, but she felt lit up from the inside.

"My folks wouldn't have it any other way," he said in a teasing tone.

As silence stretched out between them, Rachel decided to seize the moment.

She'd been waiting for a quiet moment with Gabriel so she could explain everything to him about her abrupt departure from Owl Creek. There was no time like the present.

"I owe you the truth, Gabriel. It's been weighing on my heart for a while now. It wasn't fair to run away without giving you answers."

Gabriel locked eyes with her. He didn't say a word, but he appeared to be waiting for her to continue. They both knew it had been a long time coming.

The cold wind whipped against her cheeks and she resisted the impulse to turn away. She needed to face this head-on and look him straight in the eye. It was the only way to do this with conviction. She'd had three years to prepare for this reckoning.

Lord, please help me give Gabriel closure. I've been avoiding this moment for so long.

It's time to face my truths.

"I'm sorry for the pain I caused you by leaving. I wish I'd done things differently, but I couldn't face you, Gabriel. I was a coward." She shrugged. "Maybe I couldn't take a long look in the mirror and confront the things in my past that caused me pain. I can't make up for what I did to you, but I can try to explain what happened and why I got cold feet."

Gabriel's jaw tightened. "Cold feet? Is that what you're calling it? Because to me it seemed like a lot more than that considering you ran away from the life we'd mapped out for ourselves." She winced at the hurt radiating from his eyes.

She was already making a mess of this. Nerves had taken over and she was fumbling with the right words to come clean with Gabriel. She let out a sigh, knowing she needed to get this right. They both needed to put the past behind them so they could truly move forward. "You're right. It was way more than that. When you had the accident a few weeks before the wedding, it really messed me up. It brought back all the grief and agony I felt after my dad's plane crash. It made me question marrying a pilot. It tore me up inside, thinking I would have to deal with that fear every time you flew."

"You never told me that," Gabriel rasped, his face creased in confusion.

"Yes, I did," she said in a steely tone.

"No. You didn't. I would remember if my fiancée expressed concerns about marrying me due to my being a pilot."

"Don't you remember how rattled I was after you crashed your plane? How I begged you not to fly again?" she pressed. Although she knew the fault was hers for leaving, Gabriel's denial had always been an issue. He'd never enjoyed tackling the tough subjects. It was clear to her he hadn't wanted to deal with her discomfort about the plane crash.

Gabriel frowned. "I just chalked it up to you having the jitters about me being in harm's way."

"You crashed your plane! That was *terrifying* to me."

He was staring at her with shock radiating from his eyes. It was almost as if she was speaking a foreign language to him.

"I crash-landed on Kachemak Bay. It was a textbook emergency landing. I only ended up with a few scrapes and bumps." He scratched his chin, his expression contemplative. "I do recall you being upset, but I never thought it was a deal breaker for us."

Rachel shivered and wrapped her arms around her middle. "Your accident traumatized me. It gave me flashbacks to the plane crash that killed my father. I couldn't let go of the idea that history was going to re-peat itself all over again with you."

"I'm sorry you felt that way, but the situations were totally different," he said, shaking his head.

"Not to me they weren't!" Rachel said in a raised voice. "Don't you get it? I've never gotten over losing my dad in that way. And I've never forgotten what it felt like to watch the father I loved so much crash and die right before my very eyes."

Gabriel felt shock ricochet through him. He wanted to ask her to repeat herself, but he was fairly certain he hadn't misunderstood. "What do you mean *watch*?" he asked, moving toward her so their bodies were only inches away from each other.

Rachel closed her eyes and raised her hand to her mouth. She shook her head back and forth, letting out a distressed sound.

Gabriel reached out and gently took her hands in his own. "Rachel, what are you talking about? You weren't at the hangar that day, were you?"

She looked up at him with tear-filled eyes. "Yes, I was," she admitted. "I wasn't supposed to be. I was on punishment and Mama told me I had to stay at home, but I snuck out when she went into town. All I wanted to do was to see Daddy and to tell him about how un-fair she was being to me. I needed him to hug me and tell me everything was going to be all right. Instead I ran head-on into a scene out of my worst nightmares."

Disbelief washed over him. "You saw the crash?"

Tears slid down her cheeks. She let out an anguished

sob. "Yes. I saw him coming in for the landing and I knew right away something wasn't right. I'd watched him land dozens of times and this was different. The left side of the plane was tilting at a strange angle and it was coming in too fast before it crashed. I saw it go up in flames on impact about one thousand feet from the landing strip." She was shaking uncontrollably. "I can almost smell the fire and ash. It's stayed with me ever since."

Her voice sounded flat as she continued. "A fire truck arrived on the scene, but I knew it was too late to save him. He was gone the moment the plane crashed. And I knew nothing in my life would ever be the same again."

At the moment all Gabriel wanted to do was hold Rachel in his arms and soothe away her pain. The details were so vivid it was as if she was describing a recent event and not something from more than ten years earlier. Clearly, the tragedy was seared into her memory.

"I can't imagine how traumatic it must've been."

A shudder ran through her body. "I was in shock and filled with unbearable grief. I went straight home and didn't tell a soul I'd seen my father crash his plane."

"Not even Neil or your mother?" he asked, stunned by her confession. He couldn't imagine bearing such pain and devastation all alone. Enduring such a horrific experience would scar a person.

"Not until years later. Mama had a tough time dealing with her grief. As a family we just pushed it down and never really dealt with it. There was this tremendous void in our lives and we couldn't even talk about it or give each other comfort. It was our coping mechanism, but it splintered us apart in the end. We lost the heart of our family and we couldn't even cling to each other for comfort."

Gabriel knew the Marshall family had struggled to come to terms with losing Lance, but he hadn't fully realized the torment lurking under the surface. There had been so many things left unsaid between him and Rachel. Even though they'd planned to spend their lives together he hadn't truly known her, inside and out. Clearly, she'd hidden a huge part of herself from him. And he'd been utterly clueless.

"So are you saying you walked away from me because of the way your father died?" He wanted to make sure he fully understood the reasons she'd torn their lives apart. After all this time it was still important to him.

"What I'm saying is that I realized I couldn't marry someone who took such risks as you do, Gabriel. What you do is even more dangerous than what my dad did. He flew tourists around our little corner of Alaska on a seaplane. You're a bush pilot in addition to being a charter pilot. You fly dangerous routes all the time."

Gabriel bristled. "And I'm a pretty good one at that. I've never been involved in a crash other than that single one. If you'd stuck around Owl Creek long enough you would have found out it was due to mechanical failure and not pilot error. I wasn't at fault."

"I wasn't implying otherwise," Rachel said, her voice full of contrition. "I'm not trying to upset you or place blame on you for anything I felt at the time. I'm simply trying to come clean to you about my feelings and the reasons I left town and called off the wedding." She winced. "I've spent the last few years coming to terms with my unresolved trauma from my father's plane crash. Becoming a woman of faith has helped me more than I can put into words, along with speaking to a therapist. Being a mother showed me how to be strong and face up to my fears. But back then I was too frightened to go ahead with the wedding."

Gabriel shoved his hands in his pockets and looked at the ground. This conversation made him feel vulnerable. It brought to the surface all the pent-up emotions he'd spent years trying to stuff down.

"I do appreciate you coming clean with me, Rachel, but I wish you'd been able to talk to me back then. It could have spared us both a lot of agony." He was struggling with feelings of resentment. After the plane crash Rachel had been a bit distant, but he'd chalked it up to nervousness due to their impending wedding. Why hadn't he realized she'd been pulling away from him? Why hadn't she confided in him about her struggles?

Try as he might, he couldn't seem to win the battle against the anger bubbling under the surface.

He didn't want to feel this way. He'd thought Rachel no longer had the ability to affect him like this, but he'd been wrong. She had him all twisted up inside.

"I tried. I wanted to tell you everything I was feeling, but I couldn't," she said, her words ending on a sob. Normally a woman's tears would affect him, but he had a righteous anger in his belly. "I just wasn't strong enough."

His temples throbbed as the facts spun around in his head. He wasn't sure it would ever make sense to him. As a man who liked a certain order in his life, it was a frustrating feeling.

"I guess what bothers me the most is that you had all the choices at your disposal. I didn't make any of the decisions, yet my life was completely blown off course by the ones you made for both of us."

"I pray you can forgive me someday," Rachel said in a soft voice. "I let fear swallow me up and all of my decisions were a direct result of being afraid. It's taken me a very long time, but I've finally been able to forgive myself a little."

Silence stretched out between them. Neither one seemed to know what to say to bridge the huge divide separating them. Gabriel wasn't even certain he wanted to try. He let out a huff of air. "In my head I've forgiven you a thousand times or more, but in my heart I just can't seem to let it go. Maybe if I hadn't loved you with all of my heart it would be easier. Perhaps if a hundred years passed, I'd be able to hear all of this and feel a sense of closure, but I don't. I wanted answers from you, but this—" He threw his hands up in the air. "None of what you just said to me gives me any measure of peace."

"All I can do is apologize and pray one day you can fully accept it." Her head was bowed, and he saw tears glistening on her cheeks. "I should probably go check in on Mama and take her home. It's been a long day for her. Good night, Gabriel."

With eyes full of sadness, she took off his tuxedo

jacket and handed it to him before leaving the patio and heading back inside. As he slung the jacket over his shoulder all he could smell was the aroma of vanilla and peaches—Rachel's scent—clinging to it and serving as a potent reminder of her.

Gabriel watched as Rachel walked away from him. He'd tried his best to keep calm during their discussion, but her confession had shaken him to his core. All this time he'd wanted to know the truth about Rachel's shocking departure from Owl Creek. Never had he imagined that she'd decided not to marry him due to his career as a pilot—the one area of his life where he excelled. The only thing that made him special.

He couldn't help but wonder what might have been if she'd told him everything three years ago. Would they have managed to work their way through her doubts and gotten married? Perhaps the truth was she just hadn't been ready to commit to a future with him. Being a pilot was like breathing to him. It was as much a part of him as his brown eyes or the color of his skin. Giving up his career in order to quell Rachel's fears would have been impossible.

Perhaps it just hadn't been meant to be. Maybe she'd done him a favor.

Life was like a chain. He now knew without a shadow of a doubt that the ripples from Lance Marshall's tragic death had spread to his relationship with Rachel. Despite everything she had put him through, he couldn't help but feel sympathy for all she'd endured. Lance had been a larger-than-life figure in their small Alaskan town. He'd been the reason Gabriel had dared to dream of becoming a pilot. His death had cast a pall over Owl Creek for a very long time. The Marshall family had been torn apart by grief and loss, and he wasn't sure they would ever be the same.

Although Gabriel had only been a teenager at the time, he remembered that period in his life, mainly because he was in a relationship with Rachel and he'd looked up to Lance. Her dad had taken Gabriel up into the wild blue yonder on many occasions. The older man had taught him so much about being a pilot and chasing your dreams. He'd been his mentor and friend.

How had he not realized that Rachel had been suffering from trauma? Yes, she had been quieter and more introspective in the aftermath of her father's death, but that was to be expected after such a tragic event. Gabriel hadn't ever imagined she was struggling with PTSD. Never in a million years had he suspected she'd witnessed the tragic plane crash. It was still hard to wrap his head around.

"Hey, buddy. What's going on?" Braden walked over and clapped him on the shoulder once Gabriel came back into the house.

Braden's white shirt was unbuttoned and there was no sign of his tuxedo jacket. Having grown up with Braden, Gabriel knew he was a laid-back guy who preferred jeans and a sweatshirt to any other attire. An adventure seeker, his pal had been traveling the world for years in pursuit of adrenaline-producing activities. Climbing Mount Everest, swimming with sharks, white water rafting in Costa Rica and caving in Iceland—Braden had done it all.

Gabriel simply nodded in response to the other man's question. If he uttered a single word, he might just explode.

Braden narrowed his gaze as he looked at him. "Is everything all right? You seem a little bit shaken."

He couldn't bear to pretend anymore. He'd been doing it for years and it had taken a toll on him. For so long he'd been plastering a jovial smile on his face to mask his unhappiness. Now it felt as if it was oozing out of him all at once.

"To be perfectly honest, I'm a bit rattled."

"Anything you want to talk about? They tell me I'm a good listener."

It was hard for Gabriel to confide in anyone without fearing judgment. As much as he considered Connor and Hank to be his best friends, he didn't think either one wanted to hear a single word about Rachel. Neither one would understand his inability to completely sever ties with her and move on with his life. For so long now he'd been grieving the loss of the life he'd expected to live with Rachel at his side. It was a process he had to go through in his own time.

"I thought that I knew Rachel utterly and completely. We were together ever since our teen years. Everyone here in town would laugh when we finished each other's sentences and walked through town with our hands entwined. They said we already acted like an old married couple, and I honestly thought we were destined to walk through life together." He let out a brittle laugh. "When

I wrote my vows, I had a line in there about growing old together as our hair turned gray. Just thinking about it makes me feel like the biggest fool in the world."

"Hey. Don't be so hard on yourself. I've never been in love before, but I do remember seeing the two of you around town, joined at the hip. It looked an awful lot like the real thing to me. You were the couple everyone aspired to be like."

Gabriel winced. People in Owl Creek had always told them they were the couple most likely to end up happily married with a house full of kids. Clearly, they'd been very wrong.

"I thought we had it all," he murmured. Perhaps he'd been nothing more than a naive fool.

"Maybe you did. Just because it fell apart doesn't mean it wasn't real," Braden said, his green eyes intense.

Gabriel let his friend's words wash over him. For so long he'd been trying to discount his relationship with Rachel because it ended badly. Not all of it had been a huge mess.

"You're right. It was more genuine than anything I've ever known," he acknowledged.

It had been real. Every instinct in his body told him so. But he hadn't known his former fiancée as deeply as he'd believed. There had been secrets she'd kept from him.

"How is it possible that I'm still finding out things about her? I thought we were as entwined as two people could be. I didn't think a single thing stood between us."

"I wasn't around when she left Owl Creek, but I

know it must have torn you up inside when she took off." Braden's expression radiated sympathy.

"You don't know the half of it," Gabriel muttered.

"I'm sorry, man. That's rough."

Gabriel nodded. He knew Connor must have filled him in on some of the details about Rachel being a runaway bride.

Braden continued. "To an extent I think we all harbor secrets, things we don't feel brave enough to share with the ones we love. If you're asking me for my opinion, secrets are kept due to fear and shame."

Gabriel studied Braden. If he wasn't mistaken, the other man knew a few things about secrets himself. His presence in Owl Creek had been scant over the last four years and Gabriel suspected there was more to it than met the eye. "I've always thought of you as Connor's little brother. You've grown up a lot in the last few years."

"Life forces us all to mature, whether we like it or not." Something in the depths of Braden's eyes hinted at his own transformative experiences, but Gabriel didn't dare probe even though he was curious about what made a man walk away from a life he seemed to love. Braden wasn't giving off any vibes leading him to believe he wanted to answer any questions.

"In that case I must be as old as Moses," Gabriel quipped, trying to keep things on a lighter note. He hadn't meant to go down the rabbit trail in his discussion with Braden. Lately all he'd done was dissect the past. Frankly, he was sick of it. Now that he had finally received answers from Rachel it was time to move on.

He had always imagined if he ever got the truth from

Rachel, the weight on his shoulders would immediately ease up and his heart would feel lighter. He'd really thought he would be able to move past it.

None of it was true. Now, more than ever, he was questioning the whys and why-nots. He was still stuck in limbo. And he feared he might never find his way out.

Chapter Nine

For what felt like the hundredth time since last week, Rachel replayed her conversation with Gabriel over in her mind. She'd come to the realization that confessing all to him had done absolutely nothing to make things better. In fact, it may have made things worse between them, which caused her to feel like a colossal failure.

Gabriel had been a shadow ever since then, managing to steer clear of her when he came to work on the renovation project. Although she could hear the clear signs of work taking place, she never once saw him. It made her sad to think he was avoiding coming face-to-face with her.

It also made it incredibly awkward since he was flying them to Anchorage later this morning.

Last week Dr. Norris had placed Helene's surgery on the fast track due to a cancellation on her schedule. Although Rachel considered it a blessing, Helene had needed some convincing.

"I really wasn't prepared to have the procedure so

soon," she had said in a quivering voice. "Perhaps we're being too hasty about this." Once, Rachel would have viewed her mother as being ornery, but she now knew it was anxiety.

Rachel had pressed a comforting kiss on Helene's temple. More than anything else, her mother needed kindness and compassion. Perhaps this was the role she'd been meant to play all along. "Consider it as a blessing from above, Mama. You won't have to wait weeks and weeks to get it all over and done with."

"But who will watch Lizzy and Faith while we're in Anchorage?" she'd asked fretfully.

"Sydney is quite capable of watching the girls overnight. The girls adore her and she's really great with them. Gabriel will fly us to Anchorage where you'll have the surgery the following morning. Neil plans to meet us there so he can stay with you until you're released from the hospital. Then Gabriel will fly the two of you back home."

Rachel had reached out to her older brother and told him everything with regard to their mother's health crisis. Wanting to help out, Neil had suggested he stay with her at the hospital while Rachel returned to Owl Creek to be with the girls once the surgery had been completed.

As soon as they'd formulated a plan, Rachel had reached out to Gabriel, who'd been very accommodating yet a bit curt. She couldn't help but think he was still pondering the discussion they'd had outside on the patio.

She really couldn't blame him for being upset. It wasn't fair of her to expect him to process it in such a short time, especially after he'd been in the dark for so many years.

By the time they reached the hangar for Lawson Charters, it was fairly close to takeoff. Gabriel met them there, dressed in his standard aviator gear—brown leather jacket, an oatmeal-colored sweater and cargo pants. He greeted Helene with a warm hug and took their luggage off their hands. Helene had made a big fuss about packing all of her essentials, which meant she'd ended up using two medium-sized suitcases. Rachel hadn't fought her on it since she didn't want to rock the boat and jeopardize her decision to make the trip to Anchorage.

Rachel wasn't sure who was more nervous—her or Helene. Just the thought of getting into the small plane was causing her stomach to do crazy dips. On several occasions during the course of their relationship, Gabriel had flown them to nearby venues in Alaska such as Homer and Palmer. She had always been scared to death. She'd gripped the arm rests each and every time they experienced turbulence, fearful the plane might crash. It had been terrifying.

Maybe this time would be different, but she feared the same terror would hold her in its grip.

Lord, please grant me a spirit of confidence. I'm so grateful Mama is getting the surgery.

Please don't let fear diminish this blessing.

"I hope things won't be awkward between us—" Rachel began before being cut off by Gabriel.

"Rachel, let's just focus on getting your mother to

Anchorage so she can get better. Right now, that's what matters most."

She let out a sigh of relief. Flying was nerve-racking enough without having to deal with tension between them. For now at least, they were on the same page.

"We're going to have a great flight," Gabriel said, taking her hand and squeezing it. "I even brought some peanuts and pretzels for you." He reached into a bin and handed a few bags to Rachel, who laughed as she accepted them.

"You're safe with me. I promise," he said, his voice full of conviction.

You're safe with me. Hadn't Gabriel uttered those same words after he'd proposed to her?

And yet in the deepest regions of her heart she hadn't fully trusted in him. If she'd truly felt safe she never would have run away. That realization made her sad. Gabriel had always been trustworthy to a fault. In the end her actions said so much more about her than Gabriel. She was the broken one.

Gabriel walked them through every step of the process, explaining everything in detail before takeoff. He was calm and professional. He gave each of them a headset so he could easily communicate with them during the flight. As the plane gathered speed and took off from the runway, Rachel felt the firm pressure of Helene's hand holding her own. The roar of the engine intensified as the seaplane soared into the sky. She began doing breathing exercises and having her own private conversation with God, praying for a safe journey. Her nerves were all over the place, and she couldn't seem to stop her legs from trembling.

"If you look to the right you can see Kachemak Bay." Gabriel's steady voice flowed through the headset. "Personally speaking, it's one of the most stunning views in Alaska."

Rachel leaned toward the window and looked down at the glistening waters filled with chunks of ice and snow. It was so different seeing it from this vantage point. She'd gotten glimpses from her commercial flight, but it was nothing remotely like this. It felt so up close and personal. She had the feeling it had everything to do with Gabriel being at the controls. He still had the ability to make her feel safe when she leaned on him. She was reluctant to admit it to herself, but she still sought him out as a source of comfort.

Throughout the flight, Gabriel continued to point out locations and places of interest. The sound of his voice through the headpiece was soothing. Every time he spoke, she felt a little bit calmer. She relaxed slightly as memories of her dad flying her around Alaska washed over her. He'd been passionate about flying and had taken it upon himself to educate her and Neil about all aspects of aviation. If she closed her eyes she could picture him sitting in the cockpit in his black leather bomber jacket and Ray-Ban sunglasses. His face had always been lit up with a grin in expectation of his next adventure.

As they headed toward the Lake Hood seaplane base, Helene began to point out familiar areas she recognized on the ground. She too had taken this same flight with her husband many times over the years. Rachel sensed her mother was reliving those glory days, judging by the tender smile gracing her face. How Rachel wished she could be as centered and calm as Helene regarding the flight. She would give anything to rid herself of all the fears that left her stomach in knots.

Once Gabriel began the descent, the plane began to shudder and shake due to sudden turbulence. Rachel cried out and gripped the armrest. Fear threatened to choke her. She shut her eyes tightly and began to pray. She let out a sigh of relief when the plane stopped shuddering.

When Gabriel landed the plane, Rachel wanted to stand up and cheer. The whole experience had been a bit surreal. During the moments of turbulence, memories of her father had surrounded her, almost like a blanket of protection.

It wasn't as if her anxiety completely dissipated during the flight, but during the moments of turbulence Rachel had managed to soothe herself. She'd still feared the plane going down, but those thoughts hadn't plagued her throughout the journey. She'd had some moments where she had enjoyed the scenery and felt a connection with her father.

"I forgot," she murmured. "I can't believe I didn't remember."

"Forgot what?" Helene asked, frowning. "Did you leave something at the house?"

"I forgot how amazing it can be to be up among the clouds. It's the closest I've ever been to God. That's what Daddy always used to say." Up until this moment she'd pushed that particular memory out of her mind. "I can almost hear his big baritone voice saying it right now."

"You're absolutely right. He said the same thing to me when he took me up with him," Gabriel chimed in. "I think of it almost every time I take flight. I've never known a human being who loved to soar as much as he did."

Guilt swept over her. "I've been so focused on how he died, I really haven't spent a lot of time remembering how he lived. And how much he adored flying."

Helene nodded. "Other than being a family man, that's what he was. A pilot." She shrugged. "I've always been thankful he died doing what he loved." It was hard not to notice the wistful tone of her voice. "I'm sorry I didn't share those thoughts with you and Neil."

"It's all right. I'm thankful you're telling me now." And she meant it. A lot of the resentment she'd felt toward her mother had diminished since her return to Owl Creek. After all of these years Rachel was finally finding common ground with her and understanding the pain she'd endured as a woman who'd become a widow way too soon. As a teenager she hadn't been able to empathize fully with the scope of her mother's loss. She'd been too busy nursing her own wounds and trying to block out the horrifying images of the crash.

"Are you ladies ready to deplane?" Gabriel asked. "There's a car waiting to take us to the hospital."

Gabriel had thought of everything, even the small details that she'd completely forgotten about. If she hadn't already thought the world of him, this experience would have placed him at the top of her list. He was so genuine and caring. He possessed all the best attributes for a father and husband. She'd always known this, but at the moment the knowledge crashed over her like a tidal wave.

He was going to make an Owl Creek woman a fine husband one of these days. She imagined her mother wouldn't hesitate to let her know she'd been foolish to let him slip through her fingers. But she'd never had the heart to tell her mother the extent of her worries regarding Gabriel's profession. She hadn't ever wanted to show all of her scars from having witnessed her father's fatal crash. Even now, she knew Helene had no idea how terrified she'd been to fly to Anchorage.

"I've come too far to turn back now," Helene asserted, dragging Rachel out of her thoughts. Her mother drew herself up to her full height and puffed out her chest. "Let's do this!"

Gabriel held out his arm for Helene and she quickly grabbed hold of it. As Rachel followed behind them as they exited the plane, she offered up a special thank-you. She was filled with gratitude for reaching Anchorage safely, and most of all, for her mother's courageous attitude regarding treatment. Maybe someday she could be as brave about flying.

Thank You, Lord, for traveling mercies and for giving Mama a dose of courage. We don't know what lies ahead but I know You will be watching over all of us, including Gabriel. I'm not sure I would have been able to pull this off without him.

* * *

The next morning—after undergoing a battery of presurgical tests—Helene was wheeled into surgery at Anchorage Regional Hospital. Gabriel had shown up at the hospital not only to support Helene but to watch over Rachel, as well. No matter how conflicted he felt about her confession, he still wanted to be a pillar of strength for the family. Neil hadn't yet arrived due to a flight delay, but he was expected within the hour.

Gabriel had just taken a trip to the cafeteria and brought back sustenance for himself and Rachel. He had purchased coffees for both of them, a selection of Danishes and a few pieces of fruit. When he entered the family waiting room, she was sitting with her legs curled up under her on a love seat, her ear pressed to her cell phone. He went over and sat down on the adjacent couch, placing the items down in front of him on the table and trying not to eavesdrop on her conversation.

A few moments later he heard her say, "Thanks for the update, Sydney. I'll see you later this evening."

"Coffee?" he asked, holding out a cup to her. "I have no idea if it's any good, but it's warm and full of caffeine."

"Thanks, Gabriel. This is just what I needed." She eagerly reached for the coffee and took a lengthy sip, letting out a satisfied sound. "Mmm. This is wonderful."

"Were you checking up on the girls?" he asked. He didn't want to pry but he was curious as to how they'd fared with the new sitter. Rachel hadn't said a word about it, but he suspected last night was the first time since they'd been born that she'd been separated from them overnight.

Although she was trying to hold it together, he could see the look of distress stamped on her face. "They had a rough night, according to Sydney. She said they woke up a few times crying for me. I almost lost it until I heard them giggling in the background."

Gabriel took a swig of his coffee. "Like music to your ears."

"Indeed. I have enough to worry about with Mama." Rachel looked fragile at the moment. She had a tendency to wear all her worries on the outside. Although she and Helene had always had tension in their relationship, he knew how much Rachel loved her mother.

"She's going to be all right."

Rachel's eyes were brimming with tears. "How do you know that?"

"Because I believe all of this was meant to be. Your return to Owl Creek wasn't an accident. You're the only one who could have inspired and encouraged Helene to come here for the surgery. You and the twins. Sometimes God is in the details."

"You had a part to play in all of this too. You brought us here. I'll never be able to thank you enough for such a blessing. I know you had to reschedule some flights to accommodate us. If I haven't adequately put it into words, I'm very grateful."

He smiled at her. "I was happy to do it. It'll give Seamus an opportunity to flex his muscles a little bit and take on some of the local charter flights." Seamus O'Dowd was a new pilot he had hired a few months ago.

Although a little bit rough around the edges, Seamus was showing great potential. Frankly, he just needed someone to have faith in him. Gabriel was willing to be that person, much as Lance Marshall had believed in him.

Rachel fiddled with the coffee cup in her hands. Rather than indulging in the hot brew, she was twirling the stirrer around.

"Gabriel, I didn't like the way we left things the other night. My intention was to clear the air, not put up a wall between us. I was so wrong to leave Owl Creek without telling you the reasons why. The bottom line is, I can't ever make it right. All I can do is be truthful about how I was feeling back then."

"I'm not sure I'll ever truly understand where your head was at," Gabriel confessed. "But at least now I don't have to wonder if I simply wasn't good enough."

She let out a distressed sound. "I'm so sorry I ever made you feel that way. You were the best thing that ever happened to me. No matter what else you think of me, Gabriel, I really did love you and I wanted to marry you."

"I guess it still stings that you didn't stick around to tell me in person. Why did you have to run away?" He blurted out the question. He still felt mixed-up inside and full of frustration. "All you left behind was a brief note and your engagement ring. And a host of unanswered questions."

"I thought you might convince me to stay, and I didn't want to live under the constant fear of losing you. For a long time, my stomach had been tied up in knots and it was constantly gnawing at me. As I told you last week, I was having nightmares and panic attacks stemming from the loss of my father. I never properly grieved his death. I'm not blaming Mama, but she encouraged us to stuff those feelings down as some sort of survival mechanism." She let out a ragged sigh. "Trust me—it didn't work. Even when you bury something it's still there."

A small part of him understood what she was saying while another piece of him rioted against the notion that they couldn't have worked their way through the darkest of moments. If only Rachel had allowed him to try to fix things.

"I knew being a pilot was the most important thing in your world," she said in a quiet voice.

"You're wrong," he said, his voice sounding raspy with emotion. "You mattered to me more than anything else. I can't believe you never knew that."

"I didn't," she confessed, twisting her fingers around in a nervous gesture. "Somehow it got all tangled up with everything else and I lost sight of it."

"Well then, I guess I failed in that regard," he said. "I should have let you know you were my everything— the sun rising in the morning and the stars twinkling in the evening sky."

She reached out and touched his arm, raising goose bumps on the back of his neck in the process. Despite the crackling tension between them, her touch felt comforting.

"It's not your fault that I allowed doubts to creep in. You always made me feel loved." She released a quavering breath. "I've never felt so cherished, not before or since then."

Hearing these sentiments from Rachel touched a part of him he'd believed was dead and buried. This woman confused and confounded him. Yet whenever he was in her orbit he felt more alive than ever before. Perhaps this was why none of the women he'd dated in the past few years had been able to touch his heart.

He took this moment to ask her something he had been wondering about ever since she stepped foot back in Alaska with her precious toddlers.

"And the father of your children?" he asked. "What about him? Were you in love with him, as well?"

Rachel bit her lip as Gabriel's question crashed over her. It was such a delicate subject for her to even attempt to answer. Just thinking about her relationship with Jonathan caused a heavy sensation to press against her chest. How could she ever adequately explain the situation she'd gotten herself into with Lizzy and Faith's father when she barely understood it herself?

"No, I wasn't in love with him," she admitted with a sigh. "It's hard to admit it out loud, but I met him during a time in my life when I was feeling alone and homesick. Although my nursing career was going well, I spent so much of my time at work. I really lacked a social life. I met him on a night out at the rodeo with my girlfriends. He was a bull rider and I fell hook, line and sinker for his sweet talk." She shrugged. "I wanted so badly to feel connected to somebody. And for whatever reason, I turned to Jonathan." It hit her in the gut to realize how lost she'd been during that time.

"So he's never been a part of the girls' lives?" Gabriel asked. "Not even in the beginning?"

"No, he wasn't interested in being a father. He made it pretty clear from the moment I told him I was expecting the twins. Aside from being shocked and a bit disillusioned, I was filled with a determination to raise them on my own without leaning on him for a single thing." Her voice rang out with pride. She wiped away a stray tear that streaked down her cheek. "The truth is, he wasn't father material. Not like you would have been, Gabriel."

Raw emotion threatened to consume him. After all this time her confession still packed a solid punch. It cut through him like a knife. He'd been trying to play it cool until this very moment, but he couldn't deny the impact of her words. His feelings were all over the place. His heart was beating so fast he feared it might jump out of his chest. Every time he thought he was out, she pulled him back in.

"Rachel, I—" he began.

Just then Neil came striding into the waiting room with an intense expression etched on his face. "Rachel!" he called out to his sister, reaching her side in a few easy strides.

Rachel jumped up from her seat and threw herself into her brother's open arms. "I'm so glad you're here," she said in a choked-up voice.

"Likewise," he said before turning to greet Gabriel.

Neil Marshall had inherited his six-foot-three height and solid frame from Lance. It was a bit jarring to see the resemblance between father and son. They shook hands and Neil murmured, "Thanks for everything, Gabe. I'm so grateful for you taking care of my family and making sure they made it here."

"It was my pleasure. I know how important this is for all of you. Helene is really special to a lot of people back in Owl Creek. Myself included."

Neil nodded. He was slightly out of breath. "I asked about Mama at the front desk and I guess it was good timing because the surgeon was on her way down here." He flashed them a wide grin. "She's out of surgery and on her way to the recovery area. She said the procedure went very well."

Rachel let out a sob. "Oh, that's wonderful news. When can we see her?"

"In about an hour or so someone will come and get us," Neil explained. "You'll be able to spend some time with her before you head back home."

Rachel winced. "I wish that I could stay longer. I feel so conflicted."

"You need to get back to my nieces," Neil said, placing his arm around Rachel. "It's my turn to see things through for a while. You've been doing all the heavy lifting since you returned to Owl Creek. I know it hasn't been easy juggling Mama and the twins."

"Honestly, it's been a labor of love. Coming home has given me a renewed sense of purpose." Rachel's gaze shifted so her eyes met Gabriel's. Despite everything, he still felt connected to this woman. It wasn't anything he could even put into words, but it resonated down to his toes. But every time he remembered the pain she'd caused him, Gabriel knew with a deep certainty that he couldn't afford to go down a romantic road with Rachel again. He was drawn to her like a moth to a flame, but he was smart enough to realize he could easily get burned.

Rachel couldn't contain her relief as she entered her mother's hospital room. Neil had allowed her to see Helene first due to her impending flight back to Owl Creek. Upon entering the room, a red-haired nurse wearing cartoon-themed scrubs greeted her warmly.

"She's doing really well. We've given her some crackers and juice. Don't stay long… She's pretty fatigued." Rachel nodded as the nurse left the room.

Helene was lying against two pillows, partially propped up. She gave Rachel a wan smile. Considering she'd just had major surgery, Rachel thought she looked pretty great. As a nurse, she knew some patients didn't respond well to anesthesia and had a tough time in the recovery room. Thankfully, Helene had tolerated it well.

"How are you feeling?" she asked, taking a seat in a chair next to the bed.

"I'm doing all right," Helene said, her voice sounding raspy. Her brown skin looked a little less vibrant than usual, and her eyes had slight shadows resting underneath them. Hopefully tonight Helene could get a good night's sleep.

"Mama, I think you're the bravest person I've ever known. You're so strong to have the surgery even though you were afraid. I know how hard it is to push past fears. I've been trying to be braver now that I have Lizzy and Faith."

Helene lightly squeezed her hand. "You're wrong, baby. You are a far stronger woman than I've ever been. You brought two wonderful children into the world all by yourself."

"I'm sorry I didn't live up to your expectations of me."

Helene let out a shocked sound. "My *expectations*? What are you talking about? All I ever wanted was for you to live a life filled with love, with God and your family at the center. As far as I can see, mission accomplished. You're a wonderful mother."

"Oh, Mama. That means a lot to me. For so long now I thought you didn't like me very much," she admitted, finally acknowledging the little kernel of hurt that had been embedded inside her for decades.

Helene reached out and caressed Rachel's face with her palm. "I have loved you with an everlasting love. I'm sorry I didn't always show you affection, but after we lost your father I felt so consumed by fear that I shut down a little on the inside. I loved him with every breath of my being and it was terrifying to lose him so suddenly and completely. Like you and Gabriel, we'd known each other since we were kids. I truly couldn't conceive of a world without him in it." Her lips trembled with emotion. "As a result, I turned inward and stuffed all those emotions down into a dark hole, thinking that I was saving all of us from a world of pain."

"It's understandable, Mama. Loss is such a difficult

thing to navigate. There wasn't any manual to take you through the grieving process." Rachel couldn't imagine having to walk in her mother's shoes after suffering such a devastating loss. "I imagine you were in survival mode." She herself had been on autopilot as a single mother after birthing two premature babies.

"No, there wasn't a how-to book on surviving grief, but I should have done better," Helene confessed. "I should have encouraged you to get therapy when you told me about witnessing the accident. Back then I didn't really believe in it, probably because of the way I was raised, but I've come to realize it could have helped you. Maybe then you wouldn't have run away from Gabriel and Owl Creek."

"You're not to blame. That's all in the past. If I hadn't left Alaska my girls wouldn't exist. God had a plan for me, even when I didn't."

"Amen!" Helene said before stifling a yawn.

"Mama, we can discuss this to our hearts' content when you get back home. For now, you need to rest, and I have to head to Lake Hood so I can fly home with Gabriel." She stood up and leaned over the hospital bed so she could press a kiss on Helene's temple. "Neil is here, and he's itching to see you."

"Go catch your flight, my sweet girl. And don't fret. Gabriel will get you home to your sweethearts. He's as dependable as the sun rising in the morning."

When she reached the doorway, Rachel turned around and blew her mother a kiss. So much had changed in the past few weeks between herself and Helene. Knowing her mother was proud of her made her soul soar. In a few hours she would be reunited with Lizzy and Faith. As she walked down the hall toward the waiting room her thoughts immediately veered toward Gabriel. Mama was right. He was a man a woman could count on, come what may. Most women would view him as a keeper, although she'd tossed him aside in a moment of blindness. Once again, that knowledge caused a feeling of shame to course through her.

If only she didn't harbor so many fears about him being a bush pilot and risking his life flying into remote areas in Alaska. If only he was an accountant or a bank manager or a baker. If only she wasn't tempted to fall in love with Gabriel all over again.

Chapter Ten

The flight back to Owl Creek was as uneventful as their journey to Anchorage. Her worries regarding something happening with the flight hadn't completely abated, but Gabriel made it tolerable with his lively banter and calm vibe. She still experienced a bit of anxiety regarding the possibility of an in-flight emergency occurring. At times, random images of fire and ash flitted through her mind. Although it was an uncomfortable feeling, Rachel prayed fervently and did breathing exercises until they'd safely reached Owl Creek. Snow had begun to gently fall a few minutes before Gabriel landed the plane on the runway. Rachel soaked in the beauty of the snow-capped mountains looming in the distance and the shimmering lights emanating from the shops on Main Street. Her hometown was jaw-droppingly beautiful. There wasn't any place she'd ever been to that measured up to Owl Creek, and she knew there never would be. Lately she'd been wondering if there was a place for her here if she chose to stay.

But how could she when so much was unsettled between herself and Gabriel? Could she bear to sit by and watch if he settled down with another woman and built a family? All this time she'd thought guilt and shame were her only ties to her ex-fiancé, but in reality she wondered if her feelings for him weren't coming back to life. Or was it simply nostalgia she was feeling?

On the drive back to the house, there was a companionable silence between her and Gabriel. So much had happened in the last twenty-four hours. She imagined he was just as exhausted as she was. Not to mention he would be flying back to Anchorage tomorrow to pick up her mother and Neil. She wasn't sure a simple thank-you would ever be enough.

"Home sweet home," Gabriel said as he reached the Marshall residence and parked the car in the driveway.

"Thanks for everything," she murmured after they'd both emerged from the truck.

"You're welcome. I'm glad we headed out when we did, considering all this snow coming down. It appears we're getting a little Alaskan storm." He reached into the back and pulled out her small overnight suitcase.

She turned her face up to the sky, enjoying the feeling of the snowflakes as they landed on her eyelids. As a child she'd done this every single time it snowed. Rachel twirled around as a feeling of joy swept over her. She had so much to be thankful for on this snowy Alaskan evening. So much of the time she reined in her emotions, but for right now she wanted to celebrate. What was better than dancing in the falling snow? Strangely, she'd never done it in Denver. There was something about being back home in Owl Creek that made it all the more special.

Suddenly, Rachel felt a smacking sensation against the back of her head. She reached behind her to touch her head and felt a wet, icy spot. She stopped and whirled around as a sneaking suspicion dawned on her. "What in the world?"

She immediately spotted Gabriel standing a few feet behind her shaking snow off his gloves. It was a weak attempt at getting rid of the evidence, especially since he was doing it in plain sight.

"You didn't just hit me with a snowball!" she shouted.

Gabriel smirked at her. "I'm so sorry," he said, doubled over with laughter. "I couldn't resist. You were the perfect unsuspecting victim. Consider yourself snowballed."

"Oh really?" Rachel retorted, bending over and scooping up a mound of snow in her hands. She began to shape it into the perfect snowball. "You're in for it, Lawson!"

"No offense, but I'm not scared. You were never any good at snowball throwing even though it's practically a sport here in Owl Creek," Gabriel crowed, waving a dismissive hand at her. She let out an angry cry and threw the snowball straight at him. Much to her chagrin it landed with a plop a few feet away from him. Gabriel let out a hoot of laughter. "I guess you didn't do much snowball throwing in Colorado."

Rachel bent down and gathered an armful of snow in her arms, then went running in Gabriel's direction. Having caught him off guard, Rachel threw the mound of snow directly at him. It landed smack in the middle of his face, leaving him sputtering and wiping snow away.

He let out an awful moan and dropped to his knees in the snow. Rachel stopped in her tracks. He was hurt and it was all her fault for lobbing the icy snow mixture at him. She quickly made her way to his side, consumed by worry.

"Oh no! Gabriel! Are you all right? I didn't mean to hit you in the face." She was annoyed at herself for taking it too far. Now Gabriel had his hands covering his face. For all she knew he had snow and ice in his eyes. The rule of snowball throwing had always been not to hit someone directly in the face. She reached out and pulled his hands away from his face. "Let me help you, Gabriel." After a few agonizing seconds, he was suddenly looking at her and chuckling. Not a single thing was wrong with him!

She swatted him in the arm as he got to his feet. "You're such a faker! I thought you were hurt."

"I'm a lot tougher than that. And so are you," he said, his laughter dying off as they locked gazes. "You came back to Owl Creek with a lot more grit than when you left."

"I'd like to think I'm a better person now. Older, wiser and more grounded."

She hoped Gabriel could read between the lines without her elaborating. This version of herself would never run away from the man she loved. Not for anything in this world. The person she was today would have stood her ground and faced her fears. Or so she liked to think.

Looking into Gabriel's beautiful brown eyes almost

made her lose her train of thought. His dimples only added to his charm. They were standing so close to one another she could see his breath as he spoke and the tiny caramel flecks in his eyes. Time had only made him into a more stunning version of the man she'd loved.

"Those changes haven't gone unnoticed," he rasped. He reached out and caressed her cheek with his gloved hand. It didn't bother her at all that it was damp from the snow. It made the moment even more real.

Silence settled over them and neither one said a word for a span of a few moments.

Something intense was hovering in the air around them. She could feel it washing over her like a spring rainstorm. It was obvious that Gabriel felt it too. She could see it in his posture and the way he was looking at her. Rachel held his gaze, knowing instinctively what was coming. She didn't move an inch, for fear of messing things up. She craved this kiss more than she'd ever imagined possible.

"I've been wanting to do this for a while now," Gabriel said in a low voice as he leaned down and placed a searing kiss on her mouth. His lips moved over hers powerfully yet tenderly. Rachel felt as if her knees might buckle under the impact of this wonderful kiss. It had been so long since she'd felt Gabriel's lips against her own, she'd almost forgotten what it felt like to be kissed by him. He smelled of pine and the crisp Alaskan air. His lips tasted like cinnamon. She wanted this kiss to go on until the stars were stamped from the sky.

"Gabriel." Rachel whispered his name as the kiss deepened. She felt his hands running through her hair, but then a sudden shaft of light washed over them, causing them to slowly break apart.

They both turned toward the door where Sydney was standing with a toddler in each arm. Cries of Mama rang out like a sweet melody. Never in her girls' lives had she felt so conflicted about hearing those beloved sounds. It meant she'd been torn away from Gabriel's arms in the middle of an amazing kiss. But she'd missed the twins so much! She had to go to them.

"I'm sorry," Rachel said to Gabriel as she turned back toward him. "I have to go see the girls."

"Don't be sorry, Rachel. I understand." There was something emanating from Gabriel's eyes that made her want to invite him inside, but she needed time to greet the girls and to think about the embrace they'd just shared. What did it mean for her and Gabriel? Their relationship had shifted, yet many things between them were still in limbo. Sharing a kiss just made everything more complicated. It left her feeling confused. She knew that it was important to keep an emotional distance between them, but this tender exchange put a wrench in those plans.

She ran toward the porch, mounting the steps in record time. Scooping the girls up in her arms, she began raining kisses down on their little faces. The twins giggled and laughed as if they were being tickled. When she turned around to get one last look at Gabriel, he was already in his truck and driving off into the night. The sight of his rear lights glowing in the darkness made her wish for things she'd thought had slipped through her fingers long ago.

* * *

Morning came well before Gabriel was ready to welcome it. At the crack of dawn, he stood out on his back porch and greeted the day with a hot mug of coffee and a breathtaking view of the mountains. Seamus had agreed to take all his other local flights so he could fly to Anchorage and pick up Helene and Neil. According to Neil, his mother had received word last night that she could be released, so he planned to pick them up earlier than expected.

The kiss he'd shared last night with Rachel was weighing heavily on his mind. Although it had felt blissful in the moment, he'd known a short while later that it had been a mistake. It only served to complicate matters and neither one of them needed any more drama in their lives. They'd tried once before at the happily-ever-after and it blew up in both their faces. There was still a wide chasm between them, one he wasn't sure could ever be repaired.

He shook off thoughts of Rachel and geared himself up for his flight back to Anchorage. It would serve as a welcome distraction from his ex-fiancée and the push and pull he felt toward her.

Gabriel couldn't remember ever feeling such a sense of accomplishment as when he met up with Helene and Neil at Lake Hood to take them back home. He'd always thought flying clients to remote areas off the Alaskan grid were his most epic moments as a pilot. But he'd been wrong. Now he knew there were other experiences far more meaningful.

Gabriel had shared a quiet moment with Helene in the time before the plane took off from Lake Hood.

The area had been under a fog advisory, and they were waiting for clearance from the FAA that it was safe to fly. An exhausted Neil had already fallen asleep in his seat with a big blanket covering him up.

Helene had brought a bunch of magazines to look at during the flight. Presently, she was flipping through one of them and letting out the occasional laugh. She was wearing a bright red silk scarf around her head along with a pair of dark sunglasses and bright lipstick. Helene looked like a famous movie star in hiding, he thought with a chuckle.

"You look mighty fine for someone who just had surgery," Gabriel said, reaching out to squeeze the older woman's hand.

"I haven't dressed up in ages. I knew I wouldn't be feeling my best today, so I wanted to add a little oomph to my appearance. I must admit I've been a bit down in the dumps lately, but that's all about to change." There was a light glimmering in Helene's eyes he hadn't seen in quite some time. She was slowly but surely getting her bearings back. Focusing on her physical appearance was a huge step forward.

"I know this hasn't been easy for you, but you've shown a lot of courage by doing this."

"How could I not when Rachel and the girls are counting on me? I don't want to let them down. I did too much of it in the past," she admitted, biting her lip. "I wasn't the best mother after Lance died."

"We all fall down from time to time. We're human. You ought to forgive yourself, especially when you and Rachel seem to be so tight these days." He grinned at her. "It's been nice to watch the two of you repair your relationship."

Helene frowned. "She's still disappointed in me though. I've been so uncertain about undergoing follow-up treatment and she's been trying to convince me to go ahead with it."

"What's stopping you?" he asked, curious to hear her reasons. So far he wasn't even sure Helene had been asked to explain herself. Perhaps understanding her rationale would bring them one step closer to resolving things.

"It used to be fear, but after coming all this way and having the procedure, I don't think I'm afraid anymore." Helene sounded as if she hadn't even grasped her own feelings on the matter until this very moment.

"Does that mean you've changed your mind?" Gabriel asked, his heart beating fast with the realization that Helene had come to this decision on her own terms.

"I think it does, Gabriel," she answered with a smile.

He let out a triumphant sound that woke Neil up from his nap.

"What's going on? Is everything all right?" Neil asked, sitting straight up and wiping sleep from his eyes.

Helene patted her son on the shoulder. "Everything is wonderful, son. We're just celebrating my new lease on life."

Gabriel felt overjoyed for Helene. And for Rachel, as well. This news would bring her such a sense of relief. Although he cared about Helene's welfare, Gabriel knew he was invested largely due to Rachel. After all this time, her happiness still meant the world to him.

When they arrived in Owl Creek, Gabriel drove Helene and Neil back home. He went inside briefly to help bring Helene's belongings in the house. It was possible he also wanted to get a glimpse of Rachel and test the waters between them after the kiss they had shared last night. It had been an impulsive act on both of their parts. Twenty-four hours later he was still kicking himself for it. He'd crossed an invisible line in the sand. She had already knocked his heart around once before. He couldn't open himself up to being hurt again.

Seeing Helene settled in on her love seat in the living room with her knitting basket beside her made him feel proud that he'd played a small part in her recovery. His heart had threatened to crack wide open when Lizzy and Faith nestled up on either side of her. It was awe-inspiring to bear witness to such abiding love.

When the twins stood at his feet with their arms outstretched toward him he felt a surge of protectiveness toward these two curly-headed toddlers, the likes of which he'd never felt before. These little brown-eyed charmers had quickly snuggled their way into his heart. They were so precious and innocent. He wanted to fight all of their battles for them. There wasn't anything he wouldn't do in this world to keep them safe and sound. The random thought startled him. He was getting in way over his head.

Coming face-to-face with Rachel had been a bit strained. They were like two teenagers fumbling around each other. It was as if neither one knew how to move forward after the kiss they'd shared. Did he dare bring it up? Or would that make things even more awkward between them? Helene had been shooting them a few curious glances as if she suspected something had shifted between them during her hospital stay. In the end, neither one of them had spoken to the other about the kiss. He imagined Rachel felt as troubled about it as he did.

Gabriel went home that night feeling more conflicted than ever about Rachel.

A few days had passed since Helene's surgery. Neil had returned home to his busy life in Chicago and things were returning to normal. Helene seemed to be recuperating well. For now, she seemed to be simply enjoying quiet moments and being in the presence of Rachel, Faith and Lizzy. The playroom was almost finished. Gabriel looked around the area at what he'd accomplished. It was a beautiful room fit for two little princesses. All it needed was a few final touches. He felt a smile tugging at his lips just thinking about the twins running around this room chasing one another or playing with Legos or a dollhouse.

He was struggling a bit knowing he would no longer have any reason to come by the Marshalls' home as frequently as he'd been doing. Now that Rachel and the visiting nurse were taking constant care of Helene, he really didn't have to stop by and bring her groceries or other supplies. That knowledge didn't sit well with him.

His cell phone buzzed insistently. With a groan he reached for it, his pulse quickening when he saw his mother's number on the display. It wasn't like her to call him during a work day. Normally she was too busy at Tea Time to talk. Immediately he wondered if something had happened to his dad.

"Hey, Mama. What's going on? I'm actually working at the Marshalls' house at the moment. Is anything wrong?" he asked, hoping everything was fine.

"Gabriel! I'm on my way to Tabitha's house." He could immediately detect the strain in her voice. "She's all alone over there and having contractions that are pretty close together. Dr. Barnswell is with another patient near the mountains. I don't think she's going to make it back in time to help your sister."

"I'll be right there! I know someone who can help," he said, cutting his mother off and ending the call. His mind was racing. Tabitha had lost another baby over a year ago during a very difficult delivery. He knew this was her worst-case scenario in terms of bringing this dearly cherished baby into the world.

He raced down the hall, following the din of voices leading him toward the living room.

When he reached the doorway the scene that greeted him was heartwarming. Three generations of Marshall females were in the room enjoying each other's company. Rachel was taking her mother's blood pressure while Lizzy and Faith were dancing to a cartoon on television.

"Mama, stop wiggling," Rachel implored her. "I can't get an accurate reading if you're moving around."

"I can't help it," Helene said with a giggle. "This kiddie music is catchy."

Rachel chuckled and continued with the reading,

nodding with satisfaction. "One hundred twenty over eighty. That's really great." He must have made a sound in the doorway because Rachel turned her gaze toward him.

He didn't have time to waste. His sister needed assistance only Rachel could provide at the moment. He could only pray Tabitha would be able to hold on a little bit longer.

"Rachel. I hate to bother you, but something important has come up," he called out across the room. "Can we talk for a minute?"

Rachel was at his side in a few easy strides, her pretty face creased with worry. "Is everything all right? You look a bit shaken."

"I don't think so. I just received a call from my mother. From the sounds of it, Tabitha is having contractions even though she's not due for another few weeks. To make matters worse, Doc Barnswell isn't available. I'm guessing she's a nervous wreck." His jaw clenched with emotion. "Tabitha and Gary lost a baby a year and a half ago. This is probably bringing back a lot of nightmares."

"Oh no! Is she by herself?" Concern rang out in Rachel's voice.

"Mama's on her way over there, but Gary is out of town with his band." He knew his brother-in-law would be beside himself when he got word about his wife going into labor. Gary had been doing as many gigs as he could in order to make as much money as possible before the baby arrived. That meant leaving Owl Creek and touring all over the southern portion of the state.

"How close are the contractions?" Rachel asked with a frown.

He ran a shaky hand over his face. "Mama didn't say, but it sounded like she was in a bit of discomfort." He paused for a moment, hoping he wasn't overstepping. "Do you think you could go over to the house and help her out?"

Rachel responded without hesitation. "Of course I can. I'm a nurse. It's what I'm trained for," she reassured him. "It sounds like there isn't a moment to waste." She looked at her watch then back at him. "Mama is too weak to watch the girls by herself. If you could stay here and wait for Sydney to arrive, I'll head over to Tabitha's house and check in. It's possible it's false labor. Women get Braxton-Hicks contractions all the time without being in labor."

Gabriel simply nodded. He didn't know a thing about it, but he trusted Rachel's vast knowledge on the subject. All he wanted was for his sister to safely deliver her child.

"We'll be fine," Helene called out from her chair, clearly having heard their conversation. "You need to get going, Rachel, before Tabitha delivers the baby all by her lonesome."

"She's right. I should leave now." Rachel reached down and picked up her medical bag and stuffed the blood pressure cuff inside. She grabbed her purse and keys from the table, then rushed toward the hall closet and pulled out her navy-colored winter parka. After tugging on her boots, Rachel quickly made her way to the door.

"I'll get there as soon as I can," Gabriel said, holding Faith on one hip and Lizzy on the other. "Tell Tabitha to hang in there!"

"I will," she answered before rushing outside. He watched through the window as she drove away with wheels spewing snow and ice. Although his nerves were on edge due to the unfolding situation, Gabriel felt a sense of relief in knowing Rachel was on her way to his sister's home. If anyone could guide Tabitha through what might be a tricky delivery, it was Rachel.

He just prayed his niece or nephew could wait until Rachel arrived to come into the world.

It took Rachel ten minutes flat to reach Tabitha's woodland home. Nestled near the edge of a heavily forested area, the log cabin home was charming and rustic. Smoke furled from the chimney, creating a charming scene. On numerous occasions she had been a guest at this very home, back when she'd been Gabriel's fiancée. She had always been made to feel like a welcomed guest within those walls. Being here felt a little surreal. She hadn't seen Tabitha for more than three years. For all she knew, Gabriel's sister wouldn't want to accept help from the woman who'd walked out on her baby brother.

Rachel rapped hard on the door before turning the knob and entering when she didn't hear anyone responding. She didn't have to go far before she heard Tabitha's low moans and saw Iris placing a damp cloth on her daughter's forehead. Tabitha was lying on the couch in the living room with pillows behind her back lending her support.

"Oh, Rachel. Thank the Lord you're here," Iris said when she saw her entering the room. She let out a sound of relief and stepped aside so Rachel could get closer to her daughter. Rachel pushed aside all the issues standing between her and Iris. At the moment it was all about Tabitha and her baby.

She knelt down beside the couch and held Tabitha's hand. "Gabriel sent me. He thought I might be of some help. How are you doing, Tabitha?"

"I'm all right." She winced as pain racked her body. Tabitha bore a striking resemblance to Gabriel. They'd always favored each other with their warm brown skin and dimples. Rachel had a soft space in her heart for the woman who had almost been her sister-in-law.

"Another contraction?" Rachel asked. "Let's start timing them and then I'll examine you." She was certain Tabitha was in the middle of labor. This wasn't any false alarm. Part of her job would be to keep the expectant mother calm and focused on the hard work ahead.

"Sounds good." Tabitha shot her a weak smile. "I can't believe we're seeing each other after all this time under these circumstances," she said, her breathing sounding labored. "I'm so grateful you came."

"You're welcome. Don't worry, Tabitha. I've done this a time or two. You're in good hands." She could see the look of panic on the woman's face. It wasn't easy to stay calm when you'd already lost a baby. Her examination revealed Tabitha was well on her way to delivering her baby. Rachel would do everything in her power to make sure the mom-to-be felt safe and empowered during labor.

Rachel turned around to address Iris. "Could you get me some clean towels and bring me a pair of clean scissors? If you could put the scissors in boiling water for a few minutes that would be great."

"I-Is the baby coming?" Iris asked, wringing her hands. For the first time since she'd known her, Iris looked completely ill at ease. Rachel didn't quite recognize the person standing before her. Up to this point, Gabriel's mother had always made her feel as if she was invincible.

"It won't be long now," she answered, smiling at Tabitha.

"It feels like the contractions are getting stronger," Tabitha said, groaning. "I'm scared. It's all happening so fast."

"Just breathe into them when you feel them coming," Rachel instructed. "You're almost ready to push. That's when the good stuff starts to happen," she said, keeping her voice upbeat. "In no time at all you'll be holding your baby in your arms."

"I can't believe Gary's going to miss this," Tabitha said, clearly agitated by the realization that her husband wasn't going to make it back to Owl Creek in time.

"Don't dwell on it. He'll have the rest of his life to be there for his child. That's what is most important."

By this time Iris had returned with the supplies, which she set down on the coffee table next to Rachel. Things began to move quickly once Rachel timed the contractions at three-minute intervals and Tabitha's water broke. Tabitha gave a huge effort, and after half a dozen pushes, Rachel was reaching for the baby, who let out a tremendous cry as it came into the world.

"It's a boy, Tabitha!" Rachel turned to Iris. "Would you like to cut your grandson's umbilical cord?"

"A boy!" Tabitha cried out. "Go on, Mama. Do it for Gary since he isn't here to do it himself."

Iris looked uncertain but after Tabitha's urging she proceeded to cut the cord, grinning with joy as soon as she'd done it. "Welcome to the world, grandson," she cooed, smiling down on the baby. "You're one incredible blessing from above."

Rachel quickly wrapped the baby in a blanket and placed him in Tabitha's waiting arms. The new mother looked down at her baby with an enraptured expression on her face.

"I can't believe I'm this little charmer's mama," she whispered.

"He's healthy and about as perfect as they come. If I had to guess, I'd say he's just under seven pounds," Rachel explained. "A really solid birth weight, especially since he came a bit early."

Tears slid down the new mother's cheeks as she cradled her son in her arms. She looked up at Rachel. "Thank you. I don't know what I would have done without you here by my side keeping me focused on what was coming. It's so easy to give in to fear, especially considering what happened the last time."

Rachel knew all too well how fear could paralyze a person. Tabitha hadn't given in to it even though her past experience would have given her every reason to panic. Rachel wished she had been as tenacious as

Tabitha when she'd come up against adversity in her relationship with Gabriel.

Rachel squeezed the new mother's shoulder. "You were incredible, Tabitha. And now you have a beautiful, healthy baby boy to love and nurture. Gary will be over the moon when he sees him."

"I need to call him! Mama, can you get my cell phone and put the phone on Speaker so I can give him an update?" Tabitha asked. Nodding, Iris produced the cell phone and made the call in record time.

"I'll just be outside getting some air," Rachel said, wanting to give Tabitha some privacy so she could rejoice with her husband without an audience. It was such a special time for new parents as they heralded in the arrival of their newborn.

When she reached the door, she felt a tug on her sleeve. Iris was standing there with tears pooling in her eyes.

"I can't thank you enough," the older woman said, her voice choked with emotion. "After what happened the last time, I think we were all fearing the worst. This is such a blessing."

"You don't have to thank me. This isn't the first time I've helped out with a delivery, and I hope it won't be the last. Your daughter did all the hard work. She's a trooper."

The door suddenly opened, and Gabriel was standing there looking a bit out of sorts.

He was breathing hard as if he'd run the whole way from her house. "I tried calling both of you, but no one answered. Did the baby come?"

"We were a little busy," Rachel answered in a teasing voice. "And yes, the baby has arrived safe and sound. Why don't you go check in on Tabitha? She's in the living room."

Gabriel strode toward the other room with his mother trailing behind him talking a mile a minute about her new grandchild. From her vantage point Rachel could hear his animated voice as he met his nephew. She watched as he took him in his arms and gently rocked the baby back and forth in a soothing manner. She didn't need to see his face to know it was lit up with joy. For what felt like the hundredth time since she'd been back in Owl Creek, Rachel thought about how Gabriel was made for fatherhood. He was gentle and caring, as well as loving and patient.

An uncomfortable sensation began to prick at her. She felt a little breathless watching Gabriel cradling the newborn. Rachel turned away from the sight of him and wrenched the front door open, desperate for a distraction from the heartwarming sight she hadn't been able to look away from. For the first time since she'd come home she was battling against a strong yearning. She didn't know how to put it into words, but the feeling threatened to overwhelm her. It left her feeling completely out of sorts.

She was definitely in the danger zone with Gabriel. All this time she'd been telling herself it was important to make amends with him without realizing how tricky it would be to constantly be in his presence. Memories of their relationship were everywhere. Delivering Tabitha's baby had dredged up an abundance of emotions. One year ago she had given birth to her girls without having the benefit of a partner, husband or any family members for support. Faith and Lizzy had been premature, and as a result, had needed to stay in the NICU—neonatal intensive care unit—for more than a month. Rachel had never been so scared or humbled in her life. If she hadn't been a nurse, Rachel wasn't sure how she might have coped with twin babies with health complications. It had been a time of huge stress and uncertainty.

Rachel knew she couldn't change the past, but she would have given anything to have had a strong, faithful man like Gabriel by her side as she brought her babies into the world.

Chapter Eleven

Gabriel had never seen anything as precious as his new-born nephew. God was so good! He had watched over Tabitha until Rachel could arrive at his sister's home and aid in the delivery. As a result, this amazing miniature being had come into the world, safe and sound. His sister and brother-in-law now had the family they had always dreamed of.

He was consumed by the baby and the way his adorably shaped lips were slightly moving as he clung to Gabriel's finger. He'd counted the baby's fingers and toes, marveling at how perfect he was.

"What are you going to name him?" he asked his sister, unable to tear his gaze away from her son. With his russet-colored skin and chubby cheeks, he was already a heartbreaker.

Tabitha grinned. "We decided on Casey for a boy."

"I like that. It suits him," Gabriel said, studying his nephew's face. "It's a good name. Casey Jones. Sounds like a future baseball player."

"Not many of those in these parts," Iris said with a chuckle. "He'll be a fine boy no matter what he does."

Casey began making little fussy noises and Gabriel delicately handed him back over to Tabitha. Seeing him cuddled up against her made his chest tighten with emotion. He'd once thought he would have his own children by now, but things hadn't worked out that way. Holding his nephew in his arms made the longing for his own child even more intense.

"Where's Rachel?" he asked, looking around him. He hadn't seen her since his arrival. Surely she hadn't left without saying goodbye.

"She went outside. I don't think she's come back in," Iris said. "It was an intense delivery, son. She probably just needed to take a few minutes for herself."

"I think I'm going to go outside and look for her," he told her. "She really came through for us."

His mother narrowed her gaze as she looked at him. "Are the two of you testing the waters again?" she asked, her tone blunt.

He bristled against the question. "No. Not in the way you mean. We're just friends," he said lamely. The moment the word slipped out of his mouth he knew it wasn't exactly the truth. Friends didn't share unforgettable kisses in the Alaskan moonlight. But he wasn't going to tell his mother that. Although she'd once adored Rachel, she'd become one of her harshest critics after her desertion of him.

"Are you sure? I felt something in the air between you when you arrived." Iris raised her eyebrow. Her lips were pursed. "I hope you're being careful with your heart."

"Mama! Enough!" he said, slightly raising his voice. He didn't need his mother interfering in his personal life.

Iris looked mollified. "I just don't want—"

"Me to get hurt," he interjected. "I get it. You don't have to remind me of the past. It's not something I'm likely to forget," he said in a low voice. "I'm more than capable of making my own decisions, whatever they may be."

Gabriel pushed his arms through the sleeves of his coat and went outside to look for Rachel. The door closed behind with more of a bang than he'd intended. When he walked outside he spotted her sitting on the porch steps, her eyes wide and full of questions.

"Is everything all right?" Rachel asked. "You look a little stressed out."

He shrugged off the irritation he felt toward his mother. Today was a day meant for jubilation. "Yeah. I'm fine. How could I not be? It's Casey's birthday."

"Casey, huh? That's a beautiful name for a sweet baby boy." A wistful expression was etched on her face. "I'm so thrilled for Tabitha and Gary. This baby won't ever take the place of the one they lost, but they'll cherish him all the more for what they've been through."

He went over and sat down beside her. "You played a big role in this. I can't imagine what it feels like to help bring new life into the world. You must feel like a superstar."

"It's been one of the most rewarding experiences of

my life. Most of the time in the nursing profession we deal with illness and end-of-life issues, so to bring a baby into the world and give so much joy to families always feels incredible."

"You could do a lot of good here in Owl Creek. As you've seen, your services are needed. Any chance you and the girls might stay in town?" Gabriel threw the question out casually although he felt anything but relaxed about her answer. The idea of Rachel and the twins staying in Owl Creek meant more to him than he could put into words. He'd been battling it this entire time, but he couldn't deny that Rachel and her girls were important to him.

She reached around and untied her ponytail holder then shook her dark glossy hair so it fell about her shoulders. "I don't know if I'm staying or not. When I came to town, I didn't think I'd even consider it. But being back in Owl Creek has been wonderful. Mama and I are closer than ever and she's getting stronger every day. I feel so hopeful."

"It's important that we never give up hope," Gabriel agreed, reaching out for Rachel's hand and holding it. Although it was an impulsive gesture, he didn't regret it. For so long now he'd been fighting what he was feeling for Rachel. But seeing his newborn nephew made him feel brave. A new day had dawned. "I'm rooting for you to stay. Owl Creek is much better with you and the twins in it," he said, his voice cracking with emotion.

"That's great to hear. Mama was my number-one reason for coming back, but day by day I'm finding myself rooted in this town. Knowing I could make a difference here and put my nursing degree to use is exciting. All of a sudden I feel invested in Owl Creek."

The look stamped on her face was one of pure wonder and enthusiasm. He hadn't seen this expression for quite some time, not since she'd first started nursing school. Back then she'd vowed to take the medical world by storm.

"Is that so surprising?" he asked, curious to hear her thoughts. "You did grow up here. And up until three years ago you called it home."

"In a way, yes. I never imagined coming back would feel so right. For the most part, everyone here has been wonderful to me. So much has changed in my life, but in some ways it's as if I just stepped away for a little bit and everything stayed the same here. I kind of figured the townsfolk would hate me for the way I left." She darted her gaze toward him. "Because of how I treated you and the terrible way I ended things."

He locked gazes with her. "I'm not going to let you off the hook on that one. You left me holding the bag with the church and the reception, not to mention all those flowers. It was pretty horrific." He made a face as the memory of dealing with all those painful details came flooding back. "I was stumbling around in the dark for a very long time."

Rachel cringed. "It was awful and cowardly of me. I don't think there's an apology I could make that would cover it. Just so you know, I regretted it shortly after leaving. I was in a world of pain and I really wanted to come home."

"I wish you'd come back, Rachel. Or answered the

dozens of calls I made to you. If you'd returned, who knows what might have happened?"

For a moment she didn't say anything. It seemed as if she was fumbling for the right words.

"I'm back now," she whispered, squeezing his hand. "And I'm so sorry for what I put you through."

How had he forgotten how nice it felt to sit with Rachel and hold hands? He was a simple man who wanted an uncomplicated life. Some men wanted to conquer Wall Street or run for office. All Gabriel had ever wanted was to love and be loved. And to live out his days in this magnificent Alaskan town. It was moments such as this one that meant the world to him. He'd tried to push Rachel out of his thoughts for three years, but now that she was in his orbit he was realizing she wasn't someone he wanted to forget.

"Rachel," he said in a low voice as she leaned toward him and placed a kiss on his lips. Surprise washed over him at her unexpected gesture. He returned the kiss with equal intensity, his lips moving tenderly against her own. He ran his hands through the long wavy strands of her hair as a sweet scent rose to his nostrils. He felt Rachel's hands clutching his jacket, pulling him ever closer. This kiss was proof that he hadn't just been imagining the feelings hovering beneath the surface. They were real. And from what he could see, it wasn't just one-sided.

As the kiss ended Gabriel pressed a few extra kisses on her temple and eyelids. It almost felt as if he was trying to make up for all the years they'd been apart. With a jolt he realized it just wasn't possible to fill in the gaps for that lost period of time. It was something he had to accept and completely move on from, which was easier said than done.

"I wonder if we're getting in a bit over our heads. Is it wise to go down this road when we haven't resolved the issues from the past?" she asked, ducking her head down. He could easily read her body language. Her uncertainty mirrored his own. Gabriel yearned to reassure her, despite his own doubts.

"It's not as if we're getting married," he said in a teasing voice, lifting her chin up so their eyes met.

Astonishment flared in the depths of her eyes before she threw her head back in unbridled laughter. "No, we're not," she said, "that ship kind of sailed didn't it?"

He let out a throaty chuckle. If anyone had told him he'd be laughing and joking about the wedding that wasn't with his ex-fiancée, he would have called them all kinds of crazy. But life was full of surprises. Certain moments just snuck up on a person.

This, he realized, was what he'd missed most about Rachel not being in Owl Creek.

The laughter. The light moments where everything seemed to be right in their world. Although he knew there were issues still brewing between them, for the first time they didn't seem so insurmountable. If they could share a special moment such as this one and bask in the delivery of Tabitha's son, then anything was possible.

"Tell me I'm not imagining what's happening between us," Gabriel said, needing to know he wasn't going crazy. He'd been mistaken once before about Rachel. He knew all too well how one's emotions could mess with one's head. Gabriel wanted to make sure he was seeing things clearly.

"You're not. I still feel so connected to you," Rachel acknowledged, letting out a little sigh. "I never imagined for a single moment we could get close again after everything that happened in the past."

"Neither did I, if I'm being honest," Gabriel admitted, linking his fingers through her own.

"I wasn't very mature back then. I've learned the hard way that running away never really solves anything. I like to think I've grown a lot over the past few years," Rachel said. "My triumphs have outweighed my mistakes."

"I'm really proud of how you finished your schooling and got your nursing degree."

"Finishing my studies and earning my degree was challenging," Rachel admitted. "When I left here, I headed to Colorado and crashed on a friend's couch for a few weeks. I soon realized I needed to be gainfully employed and working toward completing my coursework. So I went after it with a vengeance."

"You were always so passionate about becoming a nurse. Even when we were kids you were always patching up broken-winged birds."

"I was, wasn't I? I'd almost forgotten." She wrinkled her nose. "One Christmas my parents bought me a little medical bag and it was as if they'd bought me a ticket to the moon. I can't remember ever being so thrilled about anything."

"It's a wonderful feeling to love what you do," he

said, feeling grateful for his career as a pilot and all of the hours he'd been able to spend soaring through the air. He didn't know what he'd ever done in this world to receive such a blessing. Being a pilot was the fruition of a lifelong dream. He couldn't ask for a greater vocation, although he did wish that Rachel was on the same page as him regarding his career. He would love to see pure joy in her eyes when she was up in the air.

"It's a great day to be a nurse-midwife," she murmured, resting her head on his shoulder and letting out a sigh. He put his arm around her and leaned in. It felt good to be in this space with her where it was just the two of them. In a few minutes they would head back inside to check in on Tabitha and Casey before Rachel headed home to Helene and the girls. Tomorrow he would be back at work, flying tourists around the local area and making sure his aviation company stayed on track. But for now, he was content to savor these precious moments with Rachel.

Moments like this didn't come around very often and he intended to soak it in while it lasted. He prayed things would stay like this forever, although he feared they wouldn't. Over the past few years he'd become a realist. Life always seemed to have a way of blindsiding him when he least expected it.

The next morning, Gabriel woke up with a feeling of gratitude firmly lodged in his heart. His family had been blessed by the birth of his nephew. He'd received an early morning call from Gary raving about his baby boy. The call had been full of emotion as his brother-in-law profusely thanked him for recruiting Rachel to help out with the birth. As he'd told Gary, all the glory went to God and Rachel's midwife abilities.

Due to back-to-back clients, he didn't have time to swing by the Marshalls' house.

All he needed were a few days to complete the home renovation. He was itching to get back over there and complete the project. Who was he kidding? He really wanted to see Rachel and spend some time with her and the girls. They were all he thought about anymore other than Lawson Charters. He was determined to expand his company. There was so much potential in this region of the state. He was going to be part of a conference call tomorrow afternoon that could change everything.

He could use a favor from the big guy upstairs to bring his company to the next level. For him this new opportunity wasn't about getting wealthy or having bragging rights. It was about expanding his beloved charter outfit and bringing more jobs to Owl Creek. It would provide him with a deep sense of professional accomplishment and pride.

By the time he'd finished his charters for the day, Gabriel was wiped out and in need of a warm meal. There was a text message on his phone from Connor inviting him to have dinner at the diner with him and Hank. Even though he was exhausted, Gabriel texted back saying he would be there. He knew he'd been avoiding spending time with his two best friends because of Rachel. His budding feelings for her was something he felt protective about and he didn't want his best friends poking at it. He feared it wouldn't end well.

He swung by his house first to feed Scooby and take him for a long walk in the woods. By the time they were back home the Siberian husky was panting as if he'd run a marathon. He patted him behind the ears. "Good boy. I'll be back in a little while."

Gabriel made his way into town in fifteen minutes flat. On his way he paused to admire the town square. It was quaint and inviting with the lampposts emitting a warm glow and townsfolk bundled up to ward off the chill. He knew some people didn't care for small towns, but he loved this one with all of his heart. Hopefully one day he would get married and raise a family right here in Owl Creek. Once he'd been convinced that he would be with Rachel for the rest of his days. He'd been terribly wrong. He would hate to get his hopes up again only to be disappointed.

It would be smart to take things slow and steady considering their tangled past. Things had fallen apart before without any warning. It was a sobering thought. He'd learned the hard way that life had a way of throwing curveballs at a person.

When he entered the diner, the sounds of fifties-style music reached his ears. He grinned at the sight of Piper dancing with one of the older town residents, Lloyd Simmons. Lloyd was a widower who regularly came to the diner to bring some cheer to his life. Living alone after forty years of wedded bliss was hard to deal with for a social butterfly like Lloyd. Leave it to Piper to liven things up in the older man's world.

He paused to watch for a moment, then made his way to their usual table. Hank and Connor were already seated across from each other and involved in an animated discussion. Connor scooted over so he could sit down next to him.

"Nice to see you, Gabe. I wasn't one-hundred-percent certain you'd show up," he said, playfully jabbing him in the side.

"Where have you been hiding?" Hank asked. "We haven't seen you since the wedding."

"I'm a busy man," Gabriel answered. "I'm trying to expand my business and taking on a lot of new clients."

"Your business, huh?" Hank asked, smirking.

"I hear you've been spending a lot of time at the Marshalls' house." Connor sat back against the booth and folded his arms across his chest.

Gabriel shook his head. "You two never quit, do you? If you're hinting about Rachel then the answer is yes. We've been spending time in each other's company. And I don't want to hear any negativity about it either. I'm a grown man, and I make my own decisions." He reached for the menu and opened it with a flourish.

He could see Connor and Hank exchanging a glance.

Gabriel let out a sigh. "Just say it and be done with it. I want to enjoy my meal in peace."

Connor cleared his throat. "We just wanted to say we're sorry."

Gabriel looked back and forth between the two men. "Excuse me?"

A look of chagrin appeared on Hank's face. "We had no right to come down on you so hard about Rachel. We were just looking out for you, but the truth is, she's a good person who made a really bad decision. If you're finding a way to forgive her for it, then who are we to pass judgment?"

"Yep. That pretty much sums it up. We're the Three Amigos for life. Part of our friendship pact means supporting each other," Connor said. "No matter what."

"Wow," Gabriel said, blown away by the support of his friends. He hadn't been prepared to hear anything like this. He'd been expecting both of them to be vehemently opposed to any involvement he might have with his ex-fiancée.

"You didn't ask any questions when I forgave Sage for hiding things from everyone about her true identity," Hank explained. "You simply accepted that I loved her. We want to give you that same benefit of the doubt."

"If Rachel is the one for you, then we'll be in your corner cheering the two of you on." Connor reached over and clapped him on the shoulder. "We've got your back."

"Guys, that means the world to me, because even though we still have a lot twin work through, I think we might have a shot at finding our way back to each other," he admitted, becoming nervous as he said the words out loud. Up till this point he hadn't shared his newfound feelings for Rachel with anyone other than her. He'd spent the longest time denying it to himself. Putting it out there made him feel slightly vulnerable and scared of history repeating itself.

"Did you two discuss what went wrong last time? Her reasons for leaving?" Hank asked.

Gabriel briefly explained Rachel's fears related to his flying and how the plane crash he'd been in had deeply affected her, as well as the trauma related to her father's death.

Hank let out a low whistle. "That's really complicated. Fear is a hard thing to get a grip on."

Connor frowned at him. "So, how has it changed now? You're still a bush pilot, at least part-time. Doesn't it bother her?"

"I flew her to Anchorage for Helene's surgery and she was real jittery," Gabriel acknowledged. "She hasn't moved past the trauma related to her father's death so it might be another barrier standing between us."

"Hey! Don't sound so glum," Connor ordered. "Hank and Sage went through a lot of obstacles to be together. They're living proof that you can make it work."

"That's right! Now we just have to find someone for this guy here," Hank said, jutting his chin in Connor's direction.

Connor made a face and held up his hands. "Nope. I like being single. No one to tell me what to do or how to do it. No offense," he said, looking at Hank.

"None taken," Hank said gruffly. "Remind me to tell you I told you so when you meet your other half."

They all chuckled at the idea of Connor settling down. Even when they were kids he'd boasted about never getting married. Although he'd dated numerous women in Owl Creek, they all knew it had never been serious. Connor might very well be a lifelong bachelor. And it would suit him just fine.

By the time they placed their orders, Connor had them in stitches cracking jokes. It provided a temporary diversion from his lingering doubts about Rachel.

Gabriel's emotions were all over the place. He hated feeling so unsettled. Although it felt gratifying to have Hank and Connor's support, he still had so many reservations about the woman he'd once adored like no other. Every time he began to wrap his head around the idea of reuniting with Rachel, a warning bell began to ding in his head. It served as a reminder that he needed to tread carefully with his heart, even though he knew he'd already fallen back in love with Rachel.

Chapter Twelve

In the days following the delivery of Tabitha's baby, Rachel felt a deep sense of accomplishment. Delivering Casey had given her a feeling of purpose. There was nothing more satisfying than helping to bring a new life into the world. Her mother was recuperating nicely and seemed to be upbeat even though she was facing weeks of chemotherapy treatments. Sharing another kiss with Gabriel had given her hope that she hadn't been imagining the deepening connection between them. She couldn't help but wonder if she was falling in love with Gabriel all over again.

There had been a huge shift in the energy crackling around them. It was reminiscent of the night they'd first kissed. To her it seemed as if some of the barriers built up between them had been torn down. They'd both acknowledged what was simmering in the air between them. And it made her wish that there was a way to get past their issues. For so long she had been immersed in guilt and shame. Now she was cautiously optimistic about her future in Owl Creek. Because of Gabriel.

But it was hard to let her guard down completely. Life always had a way of disappointing her. Why did it always seem as if things got in the way between her and Gabriel? Nothing was ever simple between them. Frankly, she wondered if it ever would be. In the past she'd been terrified by the notion of losing him in a plane crash. Flying with Gabriel to Anchorage hadn't erased those fears, although it had brought back fond memories of her father's devotion to aviation. It had caused her to reflect on the joy he'd always experienced being a pilot. She knew Gabriel felt the exact same pride in his profession. Why couldn't she rid herself of this notion that Gabriel was in danger?

Lately, most of his clients had been local ones or tourists who wanted to fly over Kachemak Bay or to Denali National Park. Those flights didn't seem to have the inherent risks involved in the bush-pilot flights although there were always perils associated with flying. She still prayed about Gabriel's safety each and every day, asking the Lord to keep him free from harm. No matter how hard she tried to quell her anxiety, Rachel continued to have fears of something happening to him on one of his flights. For once, praying about her worries hadn't helped at all.

She was falling back in love with Gabriel, yet she wasn't certain if they had a future together or if he had the same growing feelings for her as well.

Rachel stepped outside on the back deck and gazed at the rugged mountains in the distance. It felt as if she could almost reach out and touch them. It was a gorgeous afternoon in Owl Creek. The sky was the glorious color of Alaskan forget-me-nots and there wasn't a cloud in sight. Even the temperature was cooperating. According to the local weatherman it was supposed to be unusually warm for November in Alaska. Rachel had convinced Helene to accompany her and the twins to the town fair featuring a book-and-bake sale. It was important to get her mother out of the house so she could interact with others. She'd also been encouraging Helene to accept visits at the house from her close friends so she wasn't cut off from the world around her.

This was the hometown she remembered, Rachel thought as they arrived at the town green. People were gathered around talking and sampling the baked goods. A crowd of kids stood around discussing whether they should go sledding or ice skating. Helene was surrounded by well-wishers. Rachel herself was deluged with townsfolk crowing over the twins. No one was shunning her or asking probing questions. A feeling of acceptance settled around her like a cozy throw.

They'd met up with Gabriel a short time after their arrival. It wasn't long before he allowed the twins to wrap him around their little fingers. He'd bought them a blueberry muffin that they were each taking turns munching on, as well as festive red balloons he'd tied to the stroller.

Her stomach did somersaults the moment Gabriel showed up looking ridiculously handsome in his green parka and jeans. Just watching him interacting with the girls gave her goose bumps. It made her realize how much her daughters could benefit from having a father figure in their lives, one who would cherish them just as much as she did herself. She'd given up on that idea a long time ago after Jonathan walked away from his responsibilities, but suddenly, hope furled inside her.

"I've been wondering when our paths would cross." The familiar voice washed over her like a warm spring rain.

When she turned around, Trudy was standing there, just as she'd expected. With her long red hair and eclectic clothes, Piper and Hank's mother was a vibrant and caring woman. She greeted Rachel with a big hug and an effervescent smile.

"It's so great to see you. Piper has been talking about you nonstop for the last few weeks. She missed you something fierce."

"Reuniting with Piper has been one of the best things about being back in Owl Creek. We picked up right where we left off." Rachel felt a grin stretching from ear to ear. She still felt thankful about her friend allowing her to make amends.

"Your twins are precious." Trudy grinned at both the girls. "My granddaughter Addie would love a playdate. They're around the same age."

"We'll have to make that happen," Rachel said, excited about the possibility of her daughters having same-aged friends in town. Although the twins had each other, socialization with other children would be so important for their development. If she decided to stay in Owl Creek, it would help them.

Trudy turned toward Gabriel. "Hank told me about

your big news," she said, clapping him on the shoulder. "It sounds very exciting."

Big news? Gabriel hadn't shared anything with her, Rachel realized with a deflated feeling.

"Is it something you're keeping under wraps?" she asked, trying not to feel a little left out. She wanted to know everything in Gabriel's world, especially the triumphs.

"Oh no! Did I say something I shouldn't have?" Trudy asked, clapping her hand over her mouth.

"Don't worry about it, Trudy," Gabriel said, his tone reassuring. "I just haven't shared it with anyone other than Hank. I just happened to run into him after I found out."

"Me and my big mouth," Trudy muttered, sending Gabriel a regretful look before she walked away.

Rachel placed Faith in the double stroller while Gabriel deposited Lizzy right in front of her. She could tell by the way they were rubbing their eyes that they were ready for a nap. Within seconds their little eyes closed and they were off to dreamland. It provided the perfect opportunity for her to press Gabriel about his news.

"So, what's going on with you?" she asked. "It sounds like congratulations are in order."

"I guess you could say that," Gabriel replied, pausing for a moment before continuing.

"I was offered a really great opportunity to partner with a company out of Homer. The corporation is called Avid Adventures. It's really going to take Lawson Charters to the next level."

"That's wonderful news! What exactly will you be

doing?" Gabriel was such a hard worker. It was always amazing when someone reaped the benefits of their long hours and dedication. She couldn't think of anyone more deserving of an opportunity to grow.

Gabriel's grin stretched wide. "Well, this company wants to pay me an exorbitant amount of money to fly wealthy clients to inaccessible areas of the state. I would be taking clients to the arctic circle, among other out-of-the-way destinations. Believe it or not, there are lots of people who crave adventures like having a pilot land on a glacier or fly them to isolated areas where there aren't even runways."

Rachel froze. A feeling of dread rose up inside her. From the sounds of it, Gabriel would be doing the most dangerous type of flying. Her throat felt dry. As the daughter of a pilot, Rachel knew the inherent risks of flying to that region. The weather itself was a challenge to pilots trying to land in that difficult terrain.

"I—I thought you were focusing more on local gigs." Rachel could barely focus. Her heart was beating like thunder inside her chest. All she kept thinking about was the fact that Gabriel would be far away from Owl Creek flying into challenging weather scenarios in off-the-grid locales.

"I was, but then this venture was placed in my lap. It's an incredible offer. With the type of salary they're offering I can really put some money into expanding Lawson Charters. I'll be able to buy a new seaplane and hire some more staff."

She allowed the idea of it to roll around in her head. Money wasn't everything, especially if you were pushing yourself to the limit and placing yourself in harm's way. She knew it hadn't ever been important to Gabriel to get rich. So what was this all about? A desire to live on the edge? If that was so, then they really were at odds. Over the last year she'd learned about what truly mattered—family, faith and serving her community as a nurse.

For so long she'd lived with the consequences of being afraid. She'd lost her fiancé, her hometown, family and friends. She couldn't go back to being anxious and fearful about Gabriel's safety. It would trickle down to the way she mothered her children and how she lived each and every day. It would make life stress-filled and uncertain. She owed more to her children, and to herself.

Gabriel was looking at her with an expectant expression stamped on his handsome face.

She knew he was waiting for her to congratulate him, but the words were stuck in her throat. It made her feel small to deny him such a simple pleasure, but she couldn't give him false praise. If there was even a small hope for the two of them, she had to be honest. The past had taught her that particular lesson.

"Gabriel, I know you love all aspects of flying, but this sounds dangerous to me."

Surprise flared in his eyes. "I'm a good pilot, Rachel. I know how to minimize the risks."

His tone was defensive. A tremor in his jaw drew her attention. Gabriel was probably hurt that she was raising her concerns rather than telling him she was proud of him. If only she could. If only she didn't feel so scared.

"I know that, but—"

"But what?" he asked, his tone on edge. "Why can't you trust in that?"

"Accidents happen," she spit out. "I know that all too well."

Her lips were quivering with emotion. She felt anxious merely thinking about Gabriel spending so much of his professional life flying in far-flung areas, some of which had no landing strips, challenging weather and unforgiving terrain. He would constantly be in peril.

"I worried that you hadn't moved past this. When we flew to Anchorage you were shaking like a leaf." His voice had a little bit of edge to it. "I should have known you were still stuck."

"I tried to push through it, largely due to your help and my desire for Mama to have the surgery. But I haven't been able to shake those fears, Gabriel. It's not as if I can snap my fingers and make the trauma go away. Don't you think I would if I could?"

"I'm sorry," he said, regret sounding in his tone. "I didn't mean to suggest you can just get over it, even after all these years, but I'd hoped…prayed things were different now."

She shook her head. "I am different, but I still have fears. Anxiety."

He ran a hand over his face. "I thought we were in a place where we could pick up the pieces and try to move forward."

Looking him in the eye felt like torture. "I did too, but I can't…not like this. Not when I'd have to be afraid all the time and wondering if you were safe. What kind of life would that be?"

"Are you saying you don't think you can be with me?" he asked in a hurt tone.

She looked over at the girls as they slept in their stroller. They were so innocent and trusting. She wasn't in this alone now. Any choices she made would affect Lizzy and Faith. From the moment they had taken their first breaths she'd made them her first priority. "I don't see a way for us, Gabriel. Not with this standing between us."

Although she spoke the words quietly, they landed with a bang. She could see the impact of her admission in Gabriel's eyes. They were flat, as if all the light had been extinguished from them. It made her want to take back what she'd said and throw herself in his arms, but she knew nothing between them would be solved by giving in to raw emotion.

"You know how I feel about flying. Giving it up isn't a choice for me," he said, anguish echoing in his voice. "It's all I've ever wanted to do with my life. It's what I was born to do."

"I know. And you shouldn't have to," she whispered, wishing things were different. But no matter how she looked at it, Gabriel devoting so much of his time to being a bush pilot was a terrifying concept. She wanted to kick herself for going down this road with Gabriel. Why had she even allowed herself to believe in second chances? Here she was, hurting him all over again.

Gabriel looked devastated. And angry. She imagined he must have looked like this when she'd run away from

Owl Creek. That time, she'd been able to avoid looking into his eyes and seeing the heartbreak, but this time she couldn't look away. And it was killing her to see him so completely shattered.

He sucked in a deep breath. "I guess you've made yourself clear."

She nodded, not trusting herself to say another word. If she opened her mouth, she might crumble into a million little pieces. Hope was a precious commodity, and in a matter of minutes it had evaporated. No matter how much things changed, some things were still the same. It didn't matter how much she loved this man or how deeply she wanted to fix the mistakes of the past. It wasn't possible for them to be together. In order to truly move on with her life, she had to accept it just wasn't meant to be and deal with her own bruised heart.

Gabriel walked away with his shoulders down and a stunned expression on his face. He looked as if every ounce of life had been drained from him. She'd done this, she realized. Once again she had crushed Gabriel and broken his spirit.

As if on autopilot, Rachel steered the stroller down the street, pausing to chat with various townsfolk who stopped to say hello or commented on the girls. If not for what had just happened between her and Gabriel, Rachel would feel content in every way imaginable. Instead, she felt as if her world was imploding a little bit more with every step she took.

Gabriel wasn't the only one who had been torn apart. Rachel herself felt as if someone had ripped her heart out of her chest. And much like the last time, there wasn't really anything she could do but wait for it to heal, even though she feared it never would.

Gabriel had spent a restless night tossing and turning in his bed. He had replayed the scene with Rachel dozens of times in his head. None of it sat right with him. It felt as if she'd pulled the rug out from underneath him. How could he not have seen it coming? Rachel was putting obstacles in their way once again. Perhaps the truth was she just wasn't that interested in a future with him and was using this as an excuse. It was a painful realization.

He'd stepped out on a limb of faith, and as a result, he felt like the world's biggest fool.

He needed to keep himself busy so thoughts of Rachel didn't creep into his consciousness.

For him there was never any question about how to clear his head. He went to the hangar and settled himself in the cockpit of his De Havilland Beaver before taking off into the cloudy skies. It had always been like this with him, from the moment he'd earned his pilot's license. People always asked him why he flew planes. Being born and bred in Alaska made him curious to see the entire state—experiencing it by plane was the best way to see a large portion of it. From the moment he'd taken his first solo flight to Fairbanks, Gabriel had been hooked. How could he even think about giving it up? Didn't Rachel know what that would do to him? It would make him a shell of himself.

By the time he landed back at the hangar he felt a bit more centered. Life would go on as it had been doing for the past three years. He'd had joy in his life thanks to the three F's—friends, family and flying. Gabriel knew he would pick himself up again and go back to the way things were before Rachel's return to Owl Creek. But his heart would be a little bit more impenetrable now. He couldn't imagine letting anyone else in. Not ever.

When Pops asked him to bring a box over to Tea Time, he quickly agreed. As he drove past the Snowy Owl diner, he made a mental note to avoid the place this week. He didn't want to run the risk of having to face Connor and Hank. After they'd been so supportive it would be humiliating to tell them what had happened between him and Rachel.

He pushed through the doors of Tea Time, focused on delivering the supplies to his mother. Her establishment didn't open until eleven so it was empty when he entered. The scent of an assortment of teas wafted in the air along with the sweet smell of baked goods. Sadly, it wasn't enough to improve his mood. All he could think about was how foolish he'd been to even think he had a second chance with Rachel.

She'd never fought for them. He needed to keep reminding himself of that until it sank in.

Gabriel had always been the one pushing for the relationship through the hard times. Rachel had always been the one to emotionally shut down and run. Even though she hadn't physically left Owl Creek this time, she'd still bailed on him.

"Hey, Mama," he said, greeting his mother as she came into view. "Where should I put this?"

She nodded toward a storage room in the back of the

kitchen. "Stash it back there, will you?" When he came back through the kitchen, his mother looked him up and down, assessing him with a critical eye.

"Pick your chin up off the ground, son. You look like you've lost your best friend."

"It's nothing. I'm just having one of those days," he said, trying to shrug off his mood. He didn't want to tell Iris about Rachel. In many ways they'd ended before they started. Gabriel sighed. Maybe he just wasn't very good at relationships. Perhaps he would be one of those people who lived alone for the rest of his days with a dozen cats for company. He wasn't sure Scooby would like that very much though.

"Stay for a while. I'll make you a cup of tea," she offered. "That always makes things better."

Gabriel didn't have the heart to tell his mother this was one situation that wouldn't be solved over chamomile tea and scones. He gamely agreed to the tea, knowing it would make her feel better, but there really wasn't anything that could change his mood. There was a little ball of anger sitting inside his chest and chiding him for daring to risk his heart again.

A few minutes later Iris returned with a tea tray filled with a teapot, cups, saucers and pots of milk and sugar. She set it down on the table and motioned for him to take a seat. Gabriel planted himself down across from her and watched as she set the teacup and saucer in front of him, then poured tea into his cup. He didn't need to even ask about the type of tea she was serving. He'd become a little bit of an expert ever since Iris had opened the tea shop.

"Citron ginger. Am I right?" he asked. It was a game he'd been playing with his mother ever since he could remember. She would bring out a tea and he would have to guess the particular flavor. It had been a very long time since he'd failed to guess correctly. Mama had taught him well.

"Yes," she answered with a smile. "You have a keen sense of smell. Well done."

He took a long sip of the hot tea. If he hadn't been so on edge, the perfectly made brew probably would have lifted his mood.

"So what is it? Did you and Rachel have a fight?" Iris asked gently. "There's been a lot of talk around town about the two of you. I asked you before, but I'm not sure I got a straight answer. Are you reuniting?"

"No, we're not getting back together. It wasn't very realistic in the first place." He needed to stop being such a dreamer. That way he could avoid crushing disappointments like this one. He didn't want to believe in happily-ever-afters, not when he wasn't destined for one.

"You've been so content lately. It's been a relief to see you so happy. You love her, don't you?" she asked. "Don't worry, son. You can tell me. I won't judge you."

"Yes. I'm in love with her, but it doesn't change anything," he answered, ducking his head so she wouldn't see his hurt. "What kind of fool am I?" He blurted out the question. "I thought we were both on the same page regarding the future. I even dug up the engagement ring I gave her. It's been buried at the bottom of my cedar chest ever since she left." He patted his jacket pocket where the ring had been sitting ever since he'd located it. "But she's running away again, telling me she can't bear the risks involved in my being a bush pilot. But I think she doesn't want me flying at all. She hasn't moved past Lance's accident. So you see, I'm pretty much back where I started, which makes me the world's biggest sucker."

"Oh no. I'm so sorry." She reached out and touched his wrist, her gesture one of support and comfort. "Surely you can understand her fears. Her father's death was so life altering and tragic. It's bound to mess with her mentally and emotionally."

"I do empathize, but I can't give up my life's dream when it's all I've ever wanted to do. For me, it just feels as if she's trying to clip my wings. Not being a pilot would be like not breathing. And if she truly loved me, she wouldn't even ask that of me. I was willing to trust her again, yet she doesn't have much faith in me."

Iris's hand was shaking, and she placed her teacup down with a slight bang.

"Don't give up hope. Talk things through. She loves you, son. I think despite everything that happened between the two of you, she's fallen for you all over again. I could see it in her eyes at the town celebration."

More than anything else in this world, Gabriel wanted to believe what his mother was saying. But he refused to give in to romantic notions rather than deal with the crushing reality. He and Rachel weren't getting a second chance. Those dreams had withered and died.

"Even if we did find our way back to one another, how can I trust her? She walked out on me before without so much as a word of goodbye. She never fought for us. It still hurts. That's not the type of love I want or need in my life."

"That's not true. She did fight for you." She began to wring her hands in a fitful gesture. "Gabriel. There's something I should have told you a long time ago." Her lips quivered. "Rachel came back to Owl Creek a few weeks after she left."

"*What?* What do you mean she came back?" Confusion washed over him. His mother wasn't making any sense. Surely he would have known if Rachel had returned weeks after she'd left. In a town like Owl Creek it would have been headline news.

"She took the ferry over. I ran into her at the docks by accident. She was looking for you, Gabriel. I was so angry about how much she'd hurt you and the way she left you in the lurch mere days before your wedding." Iris wiped away tears with the back of her hand. "I laid into her pretty harshly." She let out an agonizing sob. "I told her you didn't want to see her and that you'd already started dating other women here in town. She turned right around and got back on the ferry. Please forgive me. I stood in the way of your happiness because I was afraid of her breaking your heart again."

Gabriel was speechless. Shock roared through him at his mother's confession. Never had he imagined his beloved mother would be capable of such deception. Up to this point she'd been the most trustworthy, upstanding person in his life. She'd kept this information from him for three long years. Had he known any of this it would have been a game changer for him and Rachel.

When he got his breathing under control, he finally spoke. "How? How could you have withheld this from me for all this time? You said nothing when my heart was breaking and I could barely breathe without feeling as if someone had kicked me in the gut. Are you telling me that you knew Rachel had regrets and wanted to fix things between us?"

She nodded. "I'm ashamed to say I did. And I'm more regretful than I can ever put into words. What I did was wrong…and cruel. And you have no idea how many times I wished that I could take it back."

Gabriel scoffed. "But you can't. Life doesn't work that way, does it?" How many times had he hoped and prayed Rachel would return? And all this time his mother had hidden the truth from him in the nastiest of ways.

His mother stayed silent save for a few sniffles. She wouldn't even look him in the eye.

In this moment he desperately needed God's guidance. The anger he felt was explosive. He closed his eyes and prayed. He had suffered so much pain and heartbreak over the past three years. He'd felt betrayed and utterly lost. His mother had been one of his closest allies. Yet she'd hurt him even more than Rachel had. Her actions had been deliberate while Rachel's had been born out of fear and anxiety. He placed his hands in prayerlike fashion in front of his face.

Dear Lord, please help me make sense of all this. Give me the strength to find some light in the darkness.

Suddenly, amidst all the thoughts racing around in his head came an uplifting realization.

Rachel had tried to make things right between them after she'd left town. She'd come back to him. It must have taken a tremendous amount of courage, he realized, to show up in Owl Creek to face him. She must have been crushed when she'd been sent away. And it meant the world to him. It made him dare to dream that things between them weren't impossible. Hope flared inside him like a beacon.

Beareth all things. Believeth all things. Hopeth all things. Endureth all things. The passage from Corinthians washed over him with the force of a strong breeze.

When he opened his eyes a feeling of calm had taken hold of him. Things had been so cloudy before, but now all he saw was a shimmering light. He wasn't giving up on Rachel and all the dreams he'd held in his heart for them because he knew now she hadn't forsaken him. She'd tried to make things right and it meant the world to him.

"I love you, Mama. And in time I will forgive you, but for now I need to find Rachel. She's my priority. If you can't accept that, I'm not sure how we're going to move forward." He stood up from the table and glared at her. "But make no mistake about it. I'm going to do whatever it takes to ensure that Rachel and I never spend another day apart as long as we live."

Chapter Thirteen

Rachel took a long sip of her coffee and gazed out the living room window. Her heart was a little banged up at the moment. All the hope she'd held in her heart for herself and Gabriel had been snuffed out. It hurt so much to lose him twice in one lifetime. Not that she'd really ever had him this second time around. Things had ended before they'd even begun. She felt a small sense of gratitude that she hadn't told Gabriel she'd fallen in love with him all over again. What good would it have done to say those words and still know you couldn't make things work? It would have been even more heart-wrenching.

You're better off, she told herself. Gabriel traveling all over Alaska and risking his life wouldn't gel with the world she was trying to create for her girls. She wanted safety and security for her two little cherubs. Getting back together with him would only have led to heartache a second time around. Hadn't she had enough to last her a lifetime? She had tried her best to be optimistic, but, in the end, their lifestyles just weren't compatible.

Even though she was trying to convince herself she'd done the right thing, a niggling voice in the back of her head disputed it. Gabriel was one in a million. Once again she had allowed fear to dictate her future. Hadn't she learned anything from the past?

She felt her mother's eyes on her like laser beams. Rachel swung her gaze toward her and furrowed her brows. "What? Do I have something on my face?" She began wiping at her nose and mouth with her hand.

Helene placed her novel down. "I'm waiting for you to tell me what's wrong." She tapped at her watch. "I don't have all day. I'm not getting any younger."

Rachel let out a sigh and told her mother everything. There was really no point in hiding it. She'd learned the hard way that harboring secrets always came back to bite a person.

"Go to him. Tell him you messed up," Helene told her. "He's a very forgiving man."

Rachel let out a groan. All she felt was regret. "You didn't see the look on his face when I told him that I couldn't deal with the risks of his job. He looked as if I'd slapped him. I can't face him, not after everything I said. It was cowardly." Tears misted in her eyes. It hurt so much to know she'd squandered her second chance with Gabriel.

Helene leaned across the table, her expression intense. "After everything you've been through, are you really going to let pride stand in your way? What do you have to lose, Rachel? Doing nothing will cost you everything."

"It already has. I've allowed fear to rob me of so much," she said in a quiet voice. The last three years had been agonizing. She'd had to rebuild her life without Gabriel at its center. Now she'd foolishly thrown away the new life they could have created together. She'd grown as a person over the course of those years, but she was still making mistakes. She was still flawed. But her faith taught her that grace was given by God to all who needed it. Wasn't she worthy of it as well? Shouldn't she give herself a little bit of forgiveness for falling short?

Helene let out a frustrated sound. "Well, what are you going to do about it? Spend another three years full of regrets and recriminations? Gnash your teeth when he falls for someone else? Or gets married?"

Ouch! Mama wasn't pulling any punches. The very thought of him ending up with someone other than herself twisted her stomach into knots.

Mama was right. Gabriel was a forgiving person. He'd shown her grace time after time.

It was a part of who he was and one of the many reasons she loved him. Perhaps he could find a way to forgive her this one last time. Maybe things weren't as bleak as she imagined.

"You're right, Mama. I can't let it happen again. Even if he tells me to get lost, I'll know I tried, right? And it's important for me to step out on a limb of faith and believe. If I'd trusted in the strength of our love the first time around, we would never have been apart."

"Right!" Helene said in a raised voice. "You deserve to be happy. Go get him."

"I am. I will." Rachel said, standing up and moving toward the hall closet. She pulled on her coat, jammed her knit hat onto her head and wrapped her thick scarf around her neck. "I have no idea where he is though. For all I know he could be in Love or Fairbanks right now."

She bit her lip. The girls were happily playing in their playpen. "Do you think you could watch the girls for a little bit? Sydney will be here in five minutes. She was going to watch the girls this afternoon so I could pick up a few things in town."

"Of course I can manage," her mother responded. "Go find my future son-in-law."

Rachel found herself giggling, buoyed by her mother's support. At the moment she felt as if anything was possible. She just needed to keep the faith. Last time she hadn't been a believer, but this time she was and it made all the difference. God was going to be with her every single moment.

With a feeling of resolve, Rachel strode away from the table, her mind whirling with the perfect words to lay her heart bare to Gabriel. She faltered for a moment as the idea crossed her mind that her plea might ring hollow. He'd withstood a lot from her and there was no guarantee he would be receptive to her sentiments. What would she do if he rejected her?

Trust in the Lord with all thine heart; and lean not unto thine own understanding. The verse from Proverbs washed over her like a powerful rainstorm. For so long Rachel hadn't trusted...not in Gabriel, not in herself and not in her future. She'd been blinded by so much fear that she hadn't been able to see her way through it.

Now she was ready to grab the brass ring. Not only for herself, but for Lizzy and Faith, as well. When she reached the front door Rachel wrenched it open, letting out a gasp as she came face-to-face with the very person she'd been determined to hunt down.

The door to the Marshall home swung open just as Gabriel raised his hand to rap on the wooden surface. Rachel was standing there all bundled up in her winter gear. A pink hat sat perched on her head, framing her beautiful face and long dark hair. For a moment they simply stared at one another. Looking into Rachel's eyes reaffirmed all the reasons he'd ended up here.

Life was made up of defining moments. This was one of them. He wasn't going to let pride or hurt feelings stand in the way of being with the woman he loved. And he did love her—in a forever type of way that wouldn't be altered by time or distance.

He was fully prepared to make any concessions he needed to convince Rachel to change her mind about their future. Although he loved being a pilot, he adored Rachel more. And Lizzy and Faith. He wanted to be a family. He wanted the white picket fence and the house filled with toys. He craved it more than he'd ever imagined possible.

Dear Lord, please grant me favor with the woman I love.

He reached out for her hand and pulled her outside, tugging the door closed behind her.

"Gabriel!" she cried out in surprise. "I can't believe you're here." Her voice sounded breathless, as if she'd been running laps.

"There's so much I want to say to you," he said, cutting to the chase. It felt as if he didn't have a moment to waste. So much time had already slipped through their fingers.

All he wanted to do was sweep Rachel up in his arms and kiss away all of her doubts.

Hopefully there would be plenty of time for kissing later. He reached out and placed his hands on either side of her face. What he saw in the depths of her eyes mirrored every emotion he was feeling.

"I was at Tea Time talking to Mama. She told me everything. You came back. You tried to fix things with me, Rachel." So much emotion was pouring out of him.

"Yes. I did come back. It didn't quite turn out as I hoped, but I loved you too much not to try." She let out a sigh. "Perhaps I should have tried harder."

"I wish you'd told me what happened, Rachel."

"I didn't want you to be at odds with your mother. She did a terrible thing, Gabriel, and it hurt me very much, but I was the one who set the wheels in motion in the first place. I never should have left you or this town. Mama just pointed out how ridiculous I've been in allowing fear to cast out love."

"'There is no fear in love; but perfect love casteth out fear: because fear hath torment. He that feareth is not made perfect in love.'" The verse from John rolled effortlessly off his lips. "You're human, sweetheart. We all make mistakes. I expect we'll make a bunch more of them, but as long as we stay true to what we feel for one another, I think we'll make it."

"Me too. I had no right to put you on the spot about your career. I love you, Gabriel. And I want to be with you, no matter what you choose to do with your job. I always want you to be safe, but I have to trust in your choices."

"I choose you. And the girls. And a life lived in love. I think my bush-pilot days are over."

Rachel let out a gasp. "*No!* You can't give it up for me. You love being a pilot. It's always been your dream ever since I can remember."

"I can still be a pilot and live out those dreams. I love being in the air and flying planes. I can still do that without traveling to remote areas. I want to come home every night to my family. I don't want to be on the other side of the state for days at a time never seeing you or the twins. That's not the life I want for us." He'd never spoken truer words. The partnership with Avid Adventures would take him away from the ones he loved and it was no longer what he wanted or needed.

"Only if you're certain about it. I don't want you to ever resent me for giving it up."

"I love you, Rachel. I can't remember a time when I didn't. I want to be with you for the rest of my days. That's what I know more than anything else. We'll figure out the rest."

"I love you too, Gabriel. When you saw me standing at the door, I was on my way to go and find you. I don't care what we have to face as long as we tackle it together." She let out a sob. "Mama's illness brought me back to Owl Creek, but I think my heart was leading me straight back to you, Gabriel. I promise I'll never let fear stand between us again."

"We're older and wiser now." He ran his thumb across her cheek, marveling that this beautiful woman loved him as much as he cherished her. "We know what it's like to live without each other and I don't think either one of us wants to go through that again."

"No, we don't. We're definitely better together than apart."

"Marry me, Rachel," he said, dropping to one knee on the snowy ground. He dug into his pocket and pulled out the red velvet box, feeling thankful he was still holding on to it.

She let out a gasp as he flipped the lid open. A beautiful sapphire surrounded by diamonds sparkled and winked at her. It was the same ring Gabriel had once placed on her finger. It was something from their past, but it would also serve as a bridge to the future. And it was perfect for Rachel. Like a beacon it heralded the future stretched out before them.

"New beginnings," Gabriel said, his face filled with expectation. "By the way, you haven't given me an answer yet. You've got me on pins and needles here."

She ran her hand across his cheek. "Oh, Gabriel, I don't know what I ever did to deserve you asking me to marry you on two separate occasions." She brushed away tears from her cheeks. "The answer is yes. A thousand times yes." Gabriel let out a whoop of joy and placed the ring on her trembling finger. Rachel pulled him to a standing position so they were on the same footing.

He dipped his head down and planted a sweeping kiss on her lips. Rachel reached up and placed her arms around his neck, pulling him even closer. When the kiss ended, she let out a sigh. "I never dreamed big enough to imagine ending up with the man of my dreams. I never really believed I'd get a second chance to make things right with you. Thank you for making my wishes come true."

He placed a kiss on her temple, inhaling the sweet, honeyed scent of her. He locked eyes with her, wanting to see her expression when he brought up the twins. "I want the girls to have my name. I want to adopt them so they'll always know without a doubt that they have a father who adores them. I know we still have to build our relationship, but I want to fill that role in their lives."

"Lizzy and Faith Lawson. I like the sound of it." Tears of happiness slid down her face. "I'm so glad they'll have you to lean on when times get rough. There's nothing more important to little girls than a father's love. And there's no better man for them to call daddy than you, Gabriel Lawson."

"Let's go tell Helene and the girls. I think this very well could be the best medicine for your mother," he said. "I have the feeling she's going to be overjoyed."

"Just like we are," Rachel whispered, beaming with contentment.

Gabriel reached out and swept her up in his arms and spun her around. When he placed her back on solid ground his arms were still laced around her waist. He brought her closer toward him so he could place a triumphant kiss on her lips in celebration of their joyful news. Rachel kissed him back with equal measure, making him the happiest man on earth.

They were living proof never to give up on your happily-ever-after.

Epilogue

It was a beautiful winter's afternoon in Owl Creek. Snow blanketed the ground and perfect snowflakes gently fell from the sky. Most Alaskans would say it was the ideal weather for a winter wedding. Gabriel appreciated blue skies and the fact that there were no storms on the horizon, but he would have married Rachel in the middle of a blizzard if need be. Earlier this morning he had seen a snowy-white owl flying above the church. According to Owl Creek folklore, it was a good sign for one's wedding day. Owls brought good fortune to brides and grooms. Or so he'd always heard.

A short while later, Gabriel stood at the front of the church in his onyx-colored tuxedo with Connor and Hank by his side. It seemed to him as if the entire town had shown up to see him and Rachel get married. He grinned at his mother who was seated in the front row next to his father, Helene and Beulah. Thankfully, he'd patched things up with his mother, who had made a tremendous effort to befriend Rachel and the twins.

His siblings were all sitting together, along with Sage, Braden and the Norths. Every pew was filled with townsfolk, from his first-grade teacher to Doc Johnson. Happiness hung in the air.

The sounds of the "Wedding March" filled the air, causing goose bumps to break out on the back of his neck. His palms were a bit moist with anticipation, although he didn't have a single reservation in the world about marrying his other half. It was way overdue. And if he had anything to say about it, they would live out the rest of their lives in loving harmony.

Lizzy and Faith walked down the aisle carrying baskets filled with forget-me-not petals.

Every now and then they would throw some petals down, then turn toward each other and giggle. Their steps were faltering but they began to speed up the moment they saw him gesturing to them. When they reached him, he drew them up in his arms and pressed a kiss to each of their cheeks. He couldn't love these precious toddlers any more than he already did, regardless of their parentage. As far as he was concerned, he would be their father for the rest of his days. They had already started to call him Dada.

He couldn't think of a bigger blessing than marrying Rachel and becoming a family.

Iris and Helene stepped forward, each taking one of the girls into their arms. Piper walked down the aisle in a peacock-blue bridesmaid dress. He let out a shudder of anticipation, knowing he would soon see his bride.

Gabriel sucked in a deep breath the moment Rachel appeared on Neil's arm, looking breathtaking in an elegant ivory gown. With every step she took, the dress sparkled and shone.

A veil swept all the way down her back but didn't hide her stunning face from view.

Although he hadn't seen the dress until this very moment, both he and Rachel had been surprised when Helene had told them she'd held on to Rachel's original dress, hoping beyond hope they would find their way back to one another. Raw emotion swept through Gabriel as Rachel neared the front of the church, moments away from standing side by side with him.

Rachel couldn't hold back the tears as she walked toward her groom. She felt beautiful in a way she'd never felt before in her life. It radiated from within. She was pledging eternity to a man who had never stopped believing in her, even when she hadn't had faith in herself. As Piper was helping her get dressed for the ceremony, her thoughts had been consumed by her father. Even though he wasn't going to be present, Rachel knew he would be there in every important way. She carried his memory with her each and every day. In remembrance of him, she had stitched one of his pilot insignias on to the underside of her gown. Although it wasn't visible to anyone, Rachel felt special knowing it was there.

Gabriel took her hand as she and Neil reached the altar. Her groom tenderly pressed a kiss on the back of her hand. As the pastor conducted the ceremony, Rachel and Gabriel never stopped clasping hands. Their gazes were fixed on each other during the entire service. It was as if no one else existed but the two of them. They were pledging themselves to one another for life. They had already been through the fire; now they intended to live in the sunlight.

When it was time to kiss his bride, Gabriel didn't hesitate for a second. This was the moment he'd been waiting for, the culmination of every hope he'd ever had for their love story. There had been dark times along the way, but this was the light at the end of the tunnel.

"It took us a long time to get to this moment, but from this point forward I won't take a single second for granted," Rachel said in a low voice to Gabriel after the kiss ended.

"Nor will I. The best is yet to come," Gabriel said, taking his wife by the hand and leading her down the aisle toward the church doors. He pushed the doors open and they walked outside, greeting the glorious Alaskan afternoon as Mr. and Mrs. Gabriel Lawson.

For so long they had been living in the shadow of the past. Now they were embracing their splendid future and there wasn't a cloud in sight.

* * * * *

If you enjoyed this story, look for Sage's story,
Her Secret Alaskan Family

Dear Reader,

Thank you for joining me on this heartwarming Alaskan journey. I really enjoyed writing Rachel and Gabriel's love story. There's something really endearing about reunion romances. I love the idea of two people falling in love all over again and seeing sparks fly after years of separation. Rachel is a woman who has made a lot of mistakes based on fear and past trauma. Gabriel's strengths lie in his ability to grant forgiveness and his optimistic outlook on life. I think true love is all about being able to forge a path together despite adversities and disappointments.

In this book I also wanted to portray a love story between a mother and daughter to show the ties that forever bind us to the ones we love. My own mother suffered from cancer, and I know how deeply it can affect a family.

I love hearing from readers! I can be found on my Author Belle Calhoune Facebook page, as well as on Twitter and my website, bellecalhoune.com.

Blessings,
Belle

WE HOPE YOU ENJOYED
THIS BOOK FROM

LOVE INSPIRED
INSPIRATIONAL ROMANCE

Uplifting stories of faith, forgiveness and hope.

Fall in love with stories where faith helps
guide you through life's challenges, and discover
the promise of a new beginning.

6 NEW BOOKS AVAILABLE EVERY MONTH!

USA TODAY bestselling author

SHEILA ROBERTS

returns with the next book in her irresistible Moonlight Harbor series, set on the charming Washington coast.

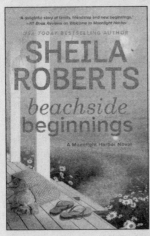

Moira Wellman has always loved makeovers—helping women find their most beautiful selves. Funny how it's taken her five years with her abusive boyfriend, Lang, to realize she needs a life makeover. When Moira finally gets the courage to leave Lang, the beachside town of Moonlight Harbor is the perfect place to start her new life.

Soon Moira is right at home, working as a stylist at Waves Salon, making new friends, saving her clients from beauty blunders and helping the women of Moonlight Harbor find the confidence to take back their lives. When she meets a handsome police officer, she's more than willing to give him a free haircut. Maybe even her heart. But is she really ready for romance after Lang? And what if her new friend is in hot pursuit of that same cop? This is worse than a bad perm. Life surely can't get any more difficult. Or can it?

With all the heart and humor readers have come to expect from a Sheila Roberts novel, _Beachside Beginnings_ is the story of one woman finding the courage to live her best life. And where better to live it than at the beach?

Coming soon from **MIRA books.**

SPECIAL EXCERPT FROM

> mira

Join USA TODAY *bestselling author Sheila Roberts for a seaside escape to the beaches of Moonlight Harbor.*

Arlene had left and Pearl had just finished trimming Jo's hair when the bell over the door of Waves Salon jingled and in walked Edie Patterson followed by a woman, who was the image of young and hip, holding a cat carrier.

"Whoa," said Jo, looking at her.

Whoa was right. The girl wore the latest style in jeans. Her jacket and gray sweater, while not high-end quality, were equally stylish. She had a tiny gold hoop threaded through one nostril, and when she flipped her hair aside part of a butterfly tattoo showed on her neck. Her features were pretty and her makeup beautifully done. And that hair. She had glorious hair—long, shimmery and luminescent like a pearl or the inside of an oyster shell. The colors were magical.

This had to be the woman Michael had sent down. Either that or she was a gift from the hair gods. She looked around the salon, taking it all in.

Pearl saw the flash of disappointment in her eyes and suddenly knew how exposed Adam and Eve must have felt after they ate that forbidden fruit. *Adam, we're naked!* Looking at her little salon through the newcomer's eyes, she saw all the things that had become invisible to her over the years: the pink shampoo bowls, old Formica styling stations, posters on the walls showing dated hairstyles like mullets and feathered bangs. The walls were the same dull cream color they'd been when Pearl had first bought the place. And the ancient linoleum floor…ugh. The place looked tired and old. With the exception of Chastity and Tyrella Lamb, who was getting her nails done, so did the women in it.

The newcomer quickly covered her disappointment with an uncertain smile.

"Hello, Pearl," said Edie. "I met this nice young lady at Nora's. She's come here looking for a job."

The woman barely waited for Edie to finish before walking up to Pearl and holding out her hand. "Hi. I'm Moira Wellman."

Determined and polite. It made a good first impression. "I'm Pearl Edwards. Michael told me you were coming."

Insecurity surfaced. The girl caught her lower lip between her teeth. "Do you have an opening? I'm good with hair," she added.

"I'm sure you are or Michael wouldn't have sent you," Pearl said. She was aware of Jo seated in her chair, taking in every word. "I tell you what. I've got a Keurig in the back room. Help yourself to some coffee and I'll be with you in just a few minutes. Okay?"

Moira nodded, picked up the cat carrier and slipped through the curtain that separated the salon from the back, where Pearl kept her supplies and washer and dryer and a small break area.

"I didn't know you were hiring someone," Jo said as Pearl returned to finish with her hair.

Pearl hadn't known she was hiring anyone, either.

Before she could speak, Chastity said, "I love her hair. I wonder if she could do that to mine."

That decided it. "I think it's time I did some updating," Pearl said.

Find out what happens next in
Beachside Beginnings
by Sheila Roberts, available April 2020 wherever
MIRA books and ebooks are sold.

MIRABooks.com

MEXPSR089